Bayou Bride

Bayou Bride

Maxine Patrick

LT

cop. 1

Thorndike Press • Thorndike, Maine

Library of Congress Cataloging in Publication Data:

Maxwell, Patricia, 1942-
   Bayou bride.

   1. Large type books.   I. Title.
[PS3563.A923B3   1981]   813'.54   81-16535
ISBN 0-89621-314-5   AACR2

Large Print edition available through arrangement with
New American Library, Inc.

Cover design by Miriam Recio.

Bayou Bride

1

Struggling with a bag of groceries, a pot of Pothos ivy, and a carton of special ice cream parfaits fast melting in the sticky heat of the June afternoon, Sherry Mason pushed the door of her small car shut. She eyed with misgivings the flight of concrete steps which led to her second story apartment. It had been quite a day. Her boss at the St. Louis office of the Villeré Shipping Lines where she worked had a broken ankle and this had been the day he decided it was time to catch up on some of the backlog of work. Since he was still laid up in bed at home, Sherry had spent the day acting more as liaison between him and the office than as a secretary. She had zipped back and forth a dozen times carrying instructions and papers to be signed. On the last trip, she had not only been caught in a traffic jam, her own car had been struck from behind. Although the damage was minor, there had been an endless wait in the hot sun for a policeman to fill out the accident report. She had spent the entire time fending off the attentions of the man who had run into her car. Returning to the office, she discovered that she had missed several telephone calls, at least two of them from Lucien Villeré, the owner of the New Orleans based shipping line. Why he should be trying to reach her, she had no idea; she could only suppose it had something to do with her employer. Her temper had been tried yet again on the way home. At the supermarket the cash register at the checkout counter had run out of tape just as she pushed her filled buggy into place beside it. No, it was not an afternoon for feats of strength; on the other hand, she just did not have the energy to make two trips up the stairs with her purchases.

Sherry was halfway to her front door when she heard the telephone. Its jangling ring inside her apartment had a persistent sound, as if the caller had no intention of being disappointed. Fishing her key from her shoulder bag, getting it in the lock and the door open, required a juggling act worthy of a circus. It was only bad luck in the form of a loose throw rug that sent the pot of ivy flying from her grasp.

"Damn," Sherry said, and annoyance was still strong in her voice as she reached for the shrilling phone and spoke into the mouthpiece.

"Miss Mason?"

"Yes?" Sherry tucked the receiver into her shoulder as she lifted the heavy bag of groceries onto the kitchen counter. The carton of parfaits needed to go into the freezer at once, but she could not quite reach it.

"Lucien Villeré. I was told at the shipping office that I might reach my brother Paul at this number."

Lucien Villeré, managing director of the Villeré Shipping Lines, a vast conglomerate with interests not only in river commerce and oceangoing freighters, but also in petroleum, large-scale farming, and sugar refining. As secretary to a minor official in the department dealing with river transport, Sherry was a small cog in an enormous piece of financial machinery. It was disconcerting to be singled out in this way. She had heard much of this man, but never spoken to him before. The deep tone of his voice with its seductive trace of a French accent was a surprise.

"Miss Mason?"

"I'm sorry, Mr. Villeré. Your brother is not here."

"When do you expect him?" The small space of time between his first question and her answer had apparently aroused suspicion in his mind. His tone indicated a tightly leashed impatience.

"I don't," Sherry replied. "I didn't know Paul was in St. Louis." Who had given this man her number? No doubt it was Sarah, the girl on the switchboard at the office. She worshiped power and men, not necessarily in that order.

The disbelief that greeted this information came strongly over the wire. As the silence stretched, Sherry frowned. What on earth had Sarah told this man? She was not left long in doubt.

"I understand that you have seen Paul often in the past few months?"

"I have gone out with him, yes," Sherry admitted. Paul Villeré was an attractive, fun-loving man with a Southern gentleman's appreciation of women. She had enjoyed his company when he was in St. Louis on business for the firm, but no more than that.

"You have been his – constant companion, in fact?"

"I don't think I would put it that way,"

Sherry began with some heat, only to be interrupted.

"Put it how you please. It is urgent that I find my brother, and I will not tolerate interference, whatever the motive. Believe me, Miss Mason, Paul has no need of your protection. Do you, or do you not, know where he can be reached?"

Sherry hung on to her temper with the greatest difficulty. "I am not protecting Paul," she said distinctly. "I have no idea where he is. I suggest you try his usual hotel."

"I have tried it, as well as a half-dozen others where he might be staying. He was not registered."

"You are certain he is in St. Louis?"

"That was the destination he gave his secretary when he asked her to make the reservations."

"Then I can only suppose he must have found accommodation elsewhere," Sherry said, her voice rising.

"My thought exactly," Lucien Villeré replied.

Sherry caught her breath at the implication of his words. He thought Paul was staying in her apartment. In business circles, Lucien Villeré had the reputation for slashing intelligence and a rapier manner which cut straight to the heart of a problem, coupled with a complete lack of either tact or mercy where the good of the firm was concerned. This, however, was carrying plain speaking too far.

Before she could form a retort scathing enough to satisfy her, he spoke again. "All I require is for you to inform my brother that I need to speak to him, and ask him to contact me as soon as possible."

"If I see him, I will certainly give him your message," Sherry said, her voice as cold as she could make it. By a supreme effort of self-control, she refrained from slamming the receiver into its cradle as she hung up on him.

Who did this man think he was? Being a multimillionaire, and in some sense her employer, did not give him the right to make insinuations about her character or her lifestyle. Simply because she lived alone and saw something of a young bachelor with the reputation of a playboy did not necessarily mean that their relationship was intimate. What kind of mind did Paul's brother have? Perhaps he judged the behavior of others by his own!

With a scowl drawing her brows together above her turquoise eyes, Sherry moved to put her ice cream away. She slammed the door of the freezer with unnecessary force before turning to the rest of her groceries.

The more Sherry thought of the telephone call, the more irritated she became. It did not matter, of course, what a man several miles away – a man whom she would probably never see – thought of her. Still, she would have given a great deal to have the opportunity back again to straighten him out. Cold hauteur was well enough, but she wished that, employer or not, she had told him what she thought of him. The slackness and low standards of the New Morality had no appeal for her. Though she covered it with an air of candor and brisk efficiency, she was basically a moonlight-and-roses girl, as old-fashioned as they came.

What had prompted the call? Was Paul in some kind of trouble that his brother was combing St. Louis for him? She would hate to think so. He had charm, did Paul Villeré. Realizing that he knew it, and capitalized upon it when he could, did not lessen her fondness for him.

There was always the possibility, of course, that the purpose of the call was a family emergency. Paul's mother was a globe-trotting widow whose greatest enjoyment of the shipping line, which she owned with her two sons, was in traveling on the freighters owned by the company. She spent months at sea every year in the company of other retired people like herself. She had started her family late in life and was no longer young. The last time Paul had mentioned her she was in the Orient, but it was always possible that she had been taken ill.

Such an explanation did not account for the fact that Paul could not be located at his usual hotel, or his failure to let his family know his whereabouts.

A long bath scented with lavender salts did much to give Sherry a new perspective on the problem. She could shake her head with a wry smile at her earlier wrath. Changing to the casual comfort of jeans and a pullover shirt, she piled her long, honey-blonde hair on top of her head for coolness and returned to the kitchen.

She ate her dinner of broiled steak and salad with unimpaired appetite. By the time she had polished off her ice cream parfait, she had very nearly regained her usual even temper.

There was a play on television she wanted to watch. She settled down to the quiet enjoyment of the story. The final credits were rolling past when the doorbell rang. She clicked off the set on the way to answer the door.

A quick look through the peephole revealed a man on her doorstep. Of medium height, he was dark. He had crisply curling black hair, brown eyes with a gleam of humor in their depths, and a small mustache over lips that were both sensitive and sensuous. It was Paul Villeré.

Frowning, Sherry swung open the door. There was an awkward moment while the smile faded from the face of the man on the doorstep.

"Don't I rate a hello?" he inquired at last.

"Hello," Sherry said.

"May I come in?"

Sherry cocked her head to one side. "Not until I have decided if you are anything at all like your brother."

"Lucien? Has he been here?"

The response was too quick, too defensive. Under Sherry's steady regard, the color deepened beneath the olive skin of Paul's face. "No," Sherry answered. "He hasn't been here, but he called."

"I can see I have some explaining to do," Paul said with a look of mock penitence.

"Yes," Sherry agreed, an irresistible smile beginning to curve her mouth. "And you can't do it on the doorstep. You may as well come in and have a cup of coffee."

"Your hospitality overwhelms me," Paul said, grinning as he stepped into the room.

"I don't suppose you have anything stronger to offer to bolster my courage."

"Afraid not."

"Then I'll have to make do with that weak stuff you call coffee. I keep telling you, if you would only come to New Orleans, I'd show you what real coffee is like."

Sherry's apartment consisted of only two rooms, a modest bedroom and a large living area that featured a sitting room at one end and a well-appointed kitchen on the other with a built-in dining nook dividing them. Paul followed her into the kitchen, where he stood leaning against the cabinet.

"Don't change the subject," Sherry told him, filling a kettle and setting it on the range top. "You were going to explain."

"First of all, tell me what Lucien said to you."

"So you can make your excuses accordingly?"

"No, so I can find out what has put you in such a rage."

Sherry turned to stare at him. "I'm not in a rage."

Paul smiled and reached out to tweak a tendril of honey-colored hair that had escaped her top knot. "No? You're as close to it as I've ever seen. I hate to sound like a grade-B movie

16

and tell you how gorgeous it makes you, but—"

"Then don't!"

"Touchy, aren't you, for somebody that's not at all hot under the collar?"

"Oh, all right," Sherry said, laughing a little, and went on to tell him what had passed between his brother and herself.

The teasing light died out of Paul's eyes, to be replaced by a frown. "I'm sorry that you were insulted," he said. "Lucien sometimes jumps to conclusions."

"Lucien," Sherry said distinctly, "is rude, arrogant, and overbearing."

"He doesn't mean to be," Paul said. "It's just his manner. Half his attitude was probably caused by his irritation with me. He doesn't approve of my leaving New Orleans at this particular time."

"So I understand, though I don't know why," Sherry said pointedly, and turned to pour the water as the kettle began to boil. Steam rose from the prepared coffeepot. Taking it up with a pair of mugs in the other hand, she moved to the dining nook and sat down at the table.

"It's a long story," Paul said, sliding into place on the bench across from her.

"I have plenty of time," Sherry said.

"It started about six years ago, the summer before I enrolled at LSU. In New Orleans, the French Creole families — that is, the families of the French people who settled in Louisiana over two hundred years ago, French men and women born outside of the mother country — have always been close. Intermarriage was a necessity in the old days, before the Americans came. Then it became a defense, and now, finally, it has achieved the status of a tradition. That's all right, as far as it goes. One of the families closest to the Villerés has always been the Dubois family. My great-grandfather went to Europe on his grand tour with a Dubois, they had plantations that marched side by side along the Mississippi. My grandfather fought in the trenches in France with a Dubois in World War I, and so it goes. Now my mother's best friend is an elderly Dubois woman who lives next door to our townhouse on the shores of Lake Pontchartrain. The summer I was nineteen, her granddaughter came to visit. She was only fourteen or fifteen, a pretty, quiet child who used to follow me around. I took her sailing on the lake, we fished, swam, water-skied, played tennis, attended a few of the dances at the country club. Aimee was incredibly sweet and gentle. I thought after a few weeks that I was in love.

18

We talked about getting married when we were older. I don't know, maybe Aimee said something to her grandmother about it. Her parents came and took her away to school in Switzerland. One day she was there, and the next she was gone. We were told we could write to each other, but you know how that goes. We exchanged letters for a while, then gradually there seemed to be less and less we had in common. After a time we stopped writing."

"Yes, I can see that," Sherry said. She poured the coffee and pushed cream and sugar toward him.

"I suppose it's a common enough story. Anyway, Aimee completed her education and then attended a finishing school. Now, after six years, she is coming home again to New Orleans. Her grandmother is giving a welcoming home party for her, and I, the faithful suitor, am expected to be on hand. Everybody seems to think that if I don't show up it's going to be like Evangeline looking for her Gabriel all over again. That Aimee is going to go into a decline like some heroine in a Victorian novel if I'm not there."

"Oh, come on," Sherry said, a smile in her eyes.

Paul had the grace to laugh at himself.

"Well, maybe it's not that bad. But words like duty and moral obligation are flying thick and fast down in New Orleans, I can tell you! If I don't watch out, I'll find myself tied to a sweet, worshipful young thing who cries if you look at her the wrong way."

Sherry sipped her coffee. "Wouldn't you like to see this girl again, at least out of curiosity?"

"Sure I would, if that was all there was to it. I'd like to see how she turned out, but I don't see why I should be bound by something I said six years ago when I was only half-grown myself."

Sherry slanted him a quick look over her coffee cup. "You did propose marriage, then?"

"I don't know," Paul said with a weary shake of his head. "I guess I must have, but who can remember after all this time? I seem to recall talking about where we would live and what we would do. Even then, Aimee wanted to buy one of these old plantation houses and modernize it, like the old Villeré Plantation Lucien fixed up as a retreat. Young as she was, Aimee knew where she wanted to live, how many children she intended to have, and whom she wanted for her husband."

"I believe you're afraid of her," Sherry teased.

Paul flung her a sardonic look. "Go ahead,

laugh," he said. "It's not your freedom that's at stake."

"No," she agreed, attempting to lift him out of his air of gloom, "but then I don't go around proposing to people."

"No," he sighed. "What I really ought to do is propose to somebody else. If I had a fiancée, Aimee would realize there was no way we could pick up where we left off. I wouldn't have to say a word."

"The only trouble with that," Sherry pointed out, "is that you would only make more trouble for yourself, since you would have another proposal to wiggle your way out of, another woman to avoid."

"True," he said, his eyes narrowing with sudden thought, "unless I proposed to you. If I asked you to marry me, Sherry, love, you wouldn't agree, would you?"

"What are you talking about?"

"You've told me often enough that I'm shallow and immature, that I take my responsibilities too lightly, and that I have precious little attraction for you as a man."

"Did I say all that?" Sherry asked, nonplussed.

"At one time or another. But you haven't answered my question. You wouldn't marry me, would you?"

"No, I don't think I would."

"Good, then you can be my fiancée!"

"You," Sherry said with a shake of her head, "are out of your mind. There is absolutely no reason to go to such lengths. This Aimee may not have any idea of holding you to your word."

"You're wrong there. She wrote her grandmother that the summer she spent with me held some of her most precious memories and that she was anxious to see me again."

"I don't see anything so terrible in that."

"Put it together with the fact that her grandmother is having the family silver — heirloom sterling — taken out of storage and polished as a gift for her granddaughter."

"That *is* a bit more damaging," Sherry admitted.

"Especially when you consider that her grandmother refused to pass the silver down to her son because he married an American girl instead of a Creole."

Sherry stared at him. "You mean Aimee has gained her grandmother's approval then with her choice? I begin to see why you're nervous."

"Nervous," Paul said, "is not the word. Let me tell you the other subtle hint I was given of what is expected of me. Last evening,

Lucien called me into the study and solemnly handed over the Villeré betrothal ring. Here, let me show you."

Paul drew a ring box of ancient, worn green velvet from his shirt pocket. Releasing the catch, he passed it across the table to Sherry. Inside was a ring set in gold so pure it had a soft rose tint. The setting was in the shape of a flower, a blue forget-me-not formed of enameled petals outlined in sapphires and dewed with diamonds.

Sherry caught her breath. "It is beautiful, so — so exquisite."

"There's a bracelet that also goes with it. The Villeré brides receive a bracelet on the day of the official announcement of the engagement. They wear both it and the ring until their wedding day, when they are replaced by something a little more modern."

"I'm not sure I would want anything more modern," Sherry said with a bemused shake of her head. She glanced up quickly. "That is, of course, if I were a Villeré bride, which I am not, nor am I going to pretend to be!"

"You are a hard woman, Sherry Mason. What would it hurt if you scheduled your vacation next week, came down to New Orleans, and let me introduce you to everyone as my bride-to-be? You could have a relaxing vacation. I would take you wherever you wanted to go, show you anything and everything you wanted to see. We could feast on seafood at some of the most famous restaurants in the world, dance, listen to jazz, take a riverboat cruise—"

"You can't be serious," Sherry interrupted. "What would I tell my boss and the people I work with? It's certain to become known that I visited New Orleans pretending to be your fiancée. I couldn't just come back and say nothing. Everybody would think— They would think we—"

"Dear Sherry, what they would think is that you came down for fun and games with me. I hadn't thought of that. What you would have to do is keep the betrothal ring, show it around at the office. Later, when it's all over, you can give it back and tell everybody it didn't work out, you couldn't take my philandering ways or something. It's not a big thing."

"It looks big to me," she told him, her eyes level. "Too big, as a matter of fact. I just couldn't go through with it. I'm no good at lying, and worse at acting a part."

Paul stared at her a long moment, then he sighed. "I was afraid of that."

"I think what you should do is call Lucien

and tell him you're on your way back home. Go to this party, see Aimee, and tell her candidly that you think the two of you should start all over. If something develops, fine; if not — well, that's fine too."

"I would hate to hurt her."

"If Aimee is the kind of person you say she is, she would prefer to be hurt now, when it can be mended, instead of later, after you were married, when it would be much harder."

The ring of the telephone cut across her words. Sherry slipped from her seat to answer it. As she lifted the receiver she glanced at the kitchen clock and was surprised to find it was nearly midnight.

"Miss Mason?"

The deep, clipped tones were unmistakable. "Yes, Mr. Villeré?" Sherry said, flicking a quick look at Paul.

"I trust I did not disturb your rest?"

"No," Sherry answered. If it had not been for the thread of purest irony in his voice she would have told him at once that Paul was with her. As it was, she waited perversely for him to ask for his brother.

"May I speak to Paul?"

The man could have at least had the diplomacy to ask whether his brother was there. His calm assumption that he was, at that time of night, was infuriating. She took a deep breath. "Your brother is here now, Mr. Villeré, but before you talk to him, I would like to clear up a misunderstanding. First of all, he arrived less than an hour ago, and second, he is not staying."

There was a small silence at the other end of the line. Finally Lucien Villeré replied, "My dear Miss Mason. Your morals are no concern of mine, and I have neither the time nor the inclination to discuss them. Would you please let me speak to Paul?"

What Lucien Villeré had said was probably no more than the exact truth. Knowing that did not help Sherry's exacerbated feelings. Not trusting herself to speak, she thrust the phone at Paul, her eyes sea-green with anger and her lovely lips pressed together.

Paul shot her a worried look before he turned his attention to the instrument in his hand. He spoke into it, then stood listening for several seconds. Sherry walked away into the living room to give him privacy and to collect herself. Behind her, she could hear Paul speaking.

"Yes, I understand the problem, but I thought she was supposed to arrive next week. All right, but I don't see why you can't pick her up, or her grandmother, for that matter.

26

What? Why would she ask for me? Well, you can suppose what you please, I can't help that. Anyway, it doesn't matter. I don't believe my fiancée would approve of me meeting a young woman, even a childhood friend, at the airport. She is the jealous type. Who? Why, Sherry Mason, of course; why else do you think I made a beeline for St. Louis as soon as I saw the way the wind was blowing—? Yes, well, sudden it may be, but that's what happens when you start putting pressure on people. You might try to remember that, Lucien."

Sherry swung around, staring at Paul. He grinned at her, unrepentant, holding out a hand to ward her off as she started toward him. Abruptly his grin faded. "What do you mean by that remark? Sherry is no particular type. She is warm and beautiful, and I'll be lucky if she consents to come anywhere near New Orleans and my family after talking to you, big brother."

The conspiratorial wink Paul threw Sherry barely registered. She stood still as Paul went on. "If you really want to know what I think, I'll tell you. I think you had better get ready to escort Aimee Dubois around for the next few weeks. Maybe she will accept a substitute. Remember you are still available in that department, old man, and I don't doubt her grandmother would be just as happy to settle for the elder son as a husband for her darling. Yes, I know you are a good twelve years her senior. Look at it this way; some girls like older men— Now, now, don't get touchy. Don't you like that trapped feeling? Despite the jokes, I am perfectly serious about one thing, Lucien. The only girl I am taking to Aimee's welcome home party is Sherry, so you had better get used to the idea!"

Sherry took a step forward. "Paul, no," she whispered, but it was a feeble denial. She could not call a halt now, could not expose the trick to Lucien Villeré's brand of cold sarcasm, or give him more reason to hold her in contempt. Every particle of pride she possessed rebelled at the idea. There was also, only partially acknowledged in a corner of her mind, a human need to repay Paul's brother in some small way for his scathing assessment of her.

Paul reached out, drawing her into the curve of his arm to give her a grateful hug. Sherry met his eyes with a wry smile, allowing him to take her silence for acquiescence, though she know with a fearful certainty that she was going to regret it.

2

Sherry leaned back on the soft seat of the air-conditioned limousine. She had never ridden in such a luxurious automobile before in her life. It was an effort to resist the impulse to smooth her fingertips over the velvet uphol-stery. If Paul was trying to impress her, he was succeeding. Not that he had any need for such measures; theirs was not that kind of re-lationship. Sending a chauffeured limousine to pick her up at the airport when he was unable to meet her plane was probably no more than a convenience to him. As pleasant as the ex-perience was, however, she would much have preferred to see Paul himself.

It had been a hectic week. At Sherry's urging, Paul had returned to New Orleans. She had even suggested that he meet Aimee when she arrived from Switzerland, as the girl wanted, in the cowardly hope that he would discover the subterfuge they had worked out was unnecessary. It did not work. Sherry had waited until half the week went by for a message telling her she need not come to New Orleans. Instead, she had received a plane ticket and the confirmation of a reservation in her name at one of the Crescent City's finest hotels.

The last thing Sherry had told Paul as he walked out the door was that she would make her own arrangements. He had laughed. His secretary would see to it, he said, and the Villeré Shipping Lines could pick up the tab. Sherry had insisted. She was due a vacation with pay. Not only could she afford to pay her own way, she preferred it. Her arguments made no difference, it appeared. It was easier to keep to the schedule set out for her than to cancel the reservations and make her own, but she was determined to have the matter out with Paul when she saw him. It might be a losing battle, trying to retain her integrity in this ridiculous situation; still, she would fight it to the end.

The prospect of asking for the time off from her job had been a daunting one. She was especially needed at this particular time, with her boss laid up in bed with a broken ankle.

The invalid was inclined to be difficult until he received at telephone call from New Orleans. The result was magical. A replacement was found within hours. Sherry had spent the last two days of the week showing the young man who took the job the small details of the position.

By that time there were some odd rumors floating about the office. Sherry had hated to wear the valuable Villeré betrothal ring, and yet it seemed preferable to allowing her reputation to be blackened, entirely due to the attention being paid to her by the head of the firm and his brother. The sight of this symbol of the mock engagement satisfied the rampant curiosity. There had been one or two spiteful comments, notably from Sarah, the receptionist who had helped start the fiasco, but most of her fellow workers were happy for her. One or two went so far as to say they had predicted the outcome weeks before.

Packing was a chore. Since she had little idea of the type of entertainments she would be expected to attend, or how formal they would be, she could not decide what to take. She had a crepe knit in a soft peach color with a chiffon drape about the shoulders that would be acceptable for the party to be given in Aimee's honor in a week's time, but other than that, she was lost. At last she opted for another long gown, a long skirt and blouse, and a collection of mixed separates. As an afterthought, she threw in jeans and a shirt. If she did not have enough, she thought her budget would stretch to one or two additions.

With that out of the way, the only thing left to be done was stop the milk delivery, clean out the refrigerator, and notify her landlady of when she would return. There was no one else to consider. Her father had been killed in an automobile accident while she was still in high school; her mother had become ill not long afterward. The diagnosis had been terminal cancer, but Sherry was not certain it should not have been grief.

The limousine left the expressway for the busy, traffic-filled streets of downtown New Orleans. With mounting excitement, Sherry recognized the broad expanse and the green-painted antique lanterns of Canal Boulevard. There was shrubbery and bright flowering annuals planted in the median, and here and there towered the shaggy heads of palm trees, a positive sign that she was in the deep south.

The car turned, entering an area of extremely narrow streets. Overhead appeared the famous wrought-iron balconies of the French Quarter, balconies that, with their supporting posts, formed an arcade above the sidewalks. Tourists strolled everywhere, most dressed in shorts, sandals, and sleeveless shirts to combat the sultry heat. They moved in and out of fascinating shops which sold everything from valuable antiques to printed T-shirts.

The limousine turned a corner. Ahead of them was an open, horse-drawn carriage decorated with flowers calmly rattling along, while closing in behind them was an enormous chartered bus with a growling engine and hissing air brakes. The contrast brought a smile to Sherry's lips. It was something of a disappointment when the limousine turned once more and pulled into the curb before the hotel.

The car door was opened not by the chauffeur, but by the hotel doorman in gold livery. As Sherry stepped out onto the sidewalk, she was assailed by the smell of seafood cooking somewhere, of coffee and the taint of horses from the carriage stand across the street from the hotel. She thanked the doorman and stood looking about her. The hotel was fronted by a series of antique brass lanterns. Its facade was constructed of white marble, inset at intervals by tall, round-arched, fanlighted windows. The effect was one of modern elegance combined with old, romantic charm.

The inside was much the same, with long stretches of gleaming marble floors overhung by enormous chandeliers glittering with crystal. Fresh flowers were here and there, calling attention to antique pieces massive enough to be in correct scale to the enormous hotel lobby. Sherry, following behind her luggage being pushed along on a cart by a bellhop, gave a slight shake of her head. The hotel was fabulous, but well beyond the pocketbook of a mere secretary. If Paul expected to find her installed here she would have to stay at least one night, but after that she would have to find other accommodation.

The clerk at the registration desk took her name. Excusing himself, he turned to the telephone, pressed a button and spoke briefly into the mouthpiece. By the time she had filled out the necessary forms, received her key, and turned to make her way to her room, a man stood beside her.

"Miss Sherry Mason? I am Jonathan Travers, the manager here," he said, giving the name of the hotel. "We are delighted to welcome you to New Orleans."

"Thank you," she replied, surprise making her tone tentative.

The manager smiled. "Lucien Villeré called to ask me to meet you. As I am sure you are aware, he would have been here to greet you himself if he could. Something came up at the last moment, but he will be with you as soon as possible."

The man had made a mistake, Sherry thought. No doubt it was Paul, not Lucien, who had called him. She saw no reason to embarrass him by correcting the wrong impression, however. "I see," she said. "I appreciate your taking the trouble to tell me."

"No trouble at all. I've known Lucien for some time. He's a great guy, a good friend. We often host business conferences, meetings, dinner parties and the like for his firm."

A small frown appeared between Sherry's eyes. If Jonathan Travers knew Lucien that well, it was unlikely that he had failed to recognize his voice on the phone. And yet she could think of no reason why Paul's older brother should concern himself with her welfare.

The manager turned away. "If you will come with me, I'll see you to your room," he said pleasantly, and led her toward a bank of elevators as the bellhop trundled her luggage behind them.

The room she had been given was done in shades of turquoise and salmon. Cool, quiet, and comfortable, it opened out onto a small roof garden enclosed on all sides by the towering walls of the hotel. As Sherry moved to the sliding glass door to inspect this secluded court with its orange trees set in boxes and its profusion of bright-colored flowers, Jonathan Travers spoke behind her.

"Is everything satisfactory?"

Sherry turned, smiling. "Oh, yes."

"I'm glad you like it. If you would care for a swim, we have a pool on the roof of the main building. There is an open air restaurant up there also. They serve a pretty fair selection of salads for lunch, if your appetite runs in that direction. Let us know where you will be if you decide to look around. We can have you paged if you have any calls."

Sherry thanked him warmly. The manager gave her a pleasant nod and left her. Sherry tipped the bellhop, who had placed her bags on the luggage racks, and he went out, closing the door behind him.

Tossing her handbag onto the bed, Sherry dropped down beside it. She was depressed. She wished fervently that she had never listened to Paul, had never abandoned her own usual good sense. What had made her do it? For the past week she had been trying to understand. She could not blame it all on overwrought nerves from her exasperating day, nor could she explain it entirely to her satisfaction as an overreaction to Lucien Villeré's negative attitude. It went further than that. She was almost convinced there had been something in the man's voice that raised her hackles, awakening an instinctive, unreasoning dislike. She wondered what it would be like when she finally met the man face to face. She had better hope, for her own peace of mind and the success of her act as Paul's fiancée, that he was just as annoying in person as he was over the phone. If he was very nice to her, she might find herself confessing the whole thing and taking the next flight back to St. Louis.

If Sherry had followed her own inclinations, she would have rested a bit, then gone out to stroll up and down the streets. That was impossible until after she had heard from Paul and discovered what his plans were. She decided at last to take the manager's suggestion. A dip in the pool and a salad for lunch it would be.

The hotel was taller than most of the older buildings around it. From the pool terrace on the top floor, she could see far out over the tiled roofs of the French Quarter. Here and there could be seen the luxuriant growth of vines climbing up the old crumbling brick walls. Pigeons wheeled overhead, landing on the rooftrees of buildings or dropping into the open squares of hidden courtyards. Beyond the houses, the Mississippi wound in a large curve, the crescent which gave the city its familiar name. As Sherry watched, a freighter slid around the bend, moving with dispatch toward its anchorage further up the river. From that distance she could not quite read the name, but she thought it was a ship of the Villeré line.

Splashing in the pool, swimming up and down, was refreshing despite the sparkle of the sun on the water. The fruit salad with cottage cheese with which she followed her exercise suited her mood and appetite to perfection. She sat for a time at one of the glass-topped metal tables, sipping the lemonade she had ordered. Only the hint of a sunburn beginning on the tops of her shoulders and across her cheekbones sent her down to her room again.

She showered, rinsing the chemicals of the pool water from her hair. Slipping on a pair of lounging pajamas in aqua silk, she combed the tangles from her long blonde tresses, and left the shining mass on her shoulders to dry. If the slight sunburn gave her an overdone look, as if she had been heavyhanded with the cheek blusher, it could not be helped. With an amused grimace, she creamed her face to prevent dryness and turned away from the mirror.

At the airport, she had bought a paperback to read on the plane. Now she took it out and sat down, quickly becoming absorbed in the story. It was sometime later when a knock fell on the door. With her book in her hand, she moved to answer it.

At the sight of the man who stood in the corridor, Sherry stiffened. Her smile of polite inquiry faded. He had the same dark coloring as Paul, the same crisp black waves and deep-set eyes under heavy dark brows. There the resemblance ended. This man was tall, with the indefinable carriage of an athlete, though dressed in a gray business suit. His face was lean and hawklike, with a bold nose and a mouth so firm it had a chiseled look. For an instant, Sherry was reminded of a comment Paul had once made concerning his brother. Lucien, he had said, was a throw-back in looks and personality to an 18th century ancestor who had founded the family fortunes by his exploits as a buccaneer upon the high seas. She had laughed then, now she felt no such inclination.

"I am Lucien Villeré," the man in the

doorway said, his black gaze flicking over the comfortable lounging costume she wore. "I see you were expecting Paul. I'm sorry that I must disappoint you."

A wave of color mounted to Sherry's face, half from embarrassment at his crude hint, half from anger at her schoolgirl reaction to it. She lifted her chin. "So am I," she said.

It was an instant before he spoke again. "Paul, unfortunately, has been called out of town. He asked me to see after you. I trust you have everything you need?"

"Yes, I believe so." The glib explanation he gave did not ring true, especially after the efforts of this man to force Paul back to the city not a week before. She could not call him a liar to his face, however, much as she might wish to. It crossed her mind to wonder if Paul had been sent out of town deliberately. She was prevented from following this line of thought to its logical conclusion as Lucien Villeré spoke again.

"Have you seen anything of New Orleans, Miss Mason?"

"Not yet," Sherry said, on guard against a sudden persuasive note she heard in his voice.

"If you will permit me, I would be honored to show you something of my city, and then we could have dinner. Paul would not like it if I left you alone on your first night here. Besides, if we are to be related, I suppose we should get to know each other better."

For some reason he meant to be conciliatory; still he could not quite keep the distaste from his voice. If he found taking her out that much of a chore, it would surely be a suitable punishment for his arrogant attitude. "I suppose we should," Sherry answered at last, her tone dry. "If you're certain it won't inconvenience you."

"Not at all," he answered, though his eyes narrowed as he stared at her. "I will return for you, shall we say in an hour?"

"I'll be ready," she replied, stepping back to close the door.

He stopped her with a gesture, his frown suddenly deepening. "Semiformal will do," he said after a moment.

"Thank you," Sherry said, and closed the door on him.

If she could have thought he was being sarcastic with his last remark, she would have been less angry. As it was, she was certain he honestly doubted that she had any idea of how to dress for dinner with someone of his social and economic standing. That was infuriating. Did he think Paul had never taken her out? Perhaps he thought his brother only carried her to quiet, out-of-the-way places!

Knowing she could not afford to stay at the hotel, Sherry had not unpacked. Now she took the assortment of evening wear she had brought with her from the suitcase and shook out the folds. Her mouth set in a grim line, she surveyed them as they lay spread upon the bed. There was the peach knit, a long gown of white eyelet, and a skirt and blouse ensemble. The knit she was saving for the party, and the white eyelet, were entirely too virginal for her mood. It would have to be the skirt and blouse. There was certainly nothing subdued about it. The skirt of cotton voile was full and long with a deep ruffle around the hem and a pattern of vivid red and turquoise flowers splashed across a white background. With it went a white voile blouse with a ruffled neckline that could be worn off the shoulder. There was also a lightweight shawl of the same material as the skirt to be draped Spanish style about the arms. The costume could be worn for a romantic effect of flowers and ruffles or, with a few adjustments, could be given dramatic flair. A militant light in her eyes, Sherry opted for the latter. If she had wished to impress Paul's family with her finer qualities and her acceptability as a wife, she would never have dreamed of being less than circumspect; as it was, the less they approved of her, the happier they would be to see the supposed engagement ended in a few weeks' time.

She brushed her hair until it shone with gold highlights before drawing it back into a low chignon on the nape of her neck. She teased soft tendril curls around her temples and before her ears, then fastened a pair of large red silk flowers on the left side of her chignon. With dark brown liner, she elongated her eyes like those of a ballerina, adding a liberal amount of turquoise shadow, and applying mascara to her lashes until they curled and began to look blatantly false. The sheer gel she applied to her lips was a brilliant red, and after a moment's consideration, she did nothing to tone down the flushed look of her cheeks. Gold hooped earrings completed the picture.

Fully dressed, Sherry stood before the mirror. She tugged the neckline of the blouse low on her arms, exposing more than a hint of the creamy curves of her breasts. She considered the addition of another silk flower on a white cord at her throat, then discarded the idea. Instead, she took up a long, gold chain from which was suspended the Villeré betrothal ring and slipped it over her head. The ring

43

nestled between her breasts, hidden beneath her blouse. She felt such a fraud wearing the ring on her finger; she much preferred this method of keeping it safe. If the effect of the concealed piece of jewelry was provocative, then that was all to the good.

Smiling a little, Sherry picked up the shawl that matched her skirt and draped it over her elbows. Turning back to the mirror, she struck a pose. Abruptly, she gave a soundless chuckle. She looked like an exotic dancer. She was not certain who would suffer more for her appearance, Lucien Villeré or herself. She adjusted the neckline of her blouse a trifle higher. It helped very little. With a resigned sigh, she reached up to remove the flowers from her hair. She was stopped by a knock on the door. She hesitated, catching her lips between her teeth, then she shrugged. Paul's brother was early. If he thought to put her at a disadvantage by such tactics he was in for a surprise — or perhaps a shock.

Lucien had also changed for dinner, trading his business suit for evening wear with a white pleated shirt that made a startling contrast to his dark, sun-bronzed skin. The only perceptible sign that he was affected by her costume was a slight tightening of his jaw muscles. "You have your key?" he asked.

"Oh, yes," she said, turning to retrieve it from the top of the dressing table. She had opened her small evening bag of antique satin to drop the key into it when he held out his hand.

"I'll take care of it for you," he said.

A strange reluctance gripped her before she shook it off. She handed the tagged key over, mentally chiding herself for that instant of primitive reaction. She knew who this man was, knew his standing in the city. There was not the least chance of danger from him.

He pressed the lock on the door from the inside, waited for her to precede him from the room, then closed the panel behind them. As they moved down the corridor, he said, "I have made our reservation at Antoine's for dinner. I hope that is satisfactory."

"Yes, very," she answered. "I've always wanted to eat there, since I read the book about the place by Frances Parkinson Keyes when I was in high school. It's one of the things I promised myself I was going to do this week." She trailed off, aware that such a show of enthusiasm did not go well with her sophisticated image.

He glanced at her. "I am glad you have a wrap then, the restaurant is only a few steps from the hotel, and there is a breeze off Lake

Pontchartrain this evening. It may get chilly later."

His stride was long. Sherry had to stretch her legs to keep up with him. The movement caused the light, flowing material of her skirt to brush against his trouser leg in a casual intimacy that she found disturbing.

In the elevator she tried to draw her skirts more closely around her, only to find his attention focused on her once more, a brooding look in his dark eyes. Unconsciously, she lifted her hand to her low bodice.

Lucien glanced away. "It is still early yet for dinner. I think a quick look at the Vieux Carré might be in order, if you have no objections?"

"I would like that," she said simply.

The Vieux Carré, the Old Square. It was the Creole name of the area of New Orleans which had once been surrounded by a walled stockade when the city had been under the French flag. Then the Spanish had come, bringing with them their tiled roof, their wrought-iron like edgings of lace, their graceful arches and galleries. They were succeeded in turn by the Americans, who with their enterprise had turned the city into a bustling, modern metropolis, but had not entirely conquered the past.

Sherry had always enjoyed history, especially in the form of historical novels. Since going to work for a firm with New Orleans offices, she had read a great deal about this uniquely foreign city on United States soil. It had assumed a fascination for her. Now it lay spread around her, filled with enchanting sights and sounds and aromas.

As they left the hotel, Lucien started toward a black Mercedes drawn up at the curb. As he reached for the passenger door, Sherry said, "Oh, couldn't we walk?"

"It may be a bit rough in those shoes," he warned with a glance at the red, spaghetti-strap sandals she wore.

"I don't mind."

"I have a better idea." He turned to hail one of the horse-drawn carriages from the stand across the street.

Sherry thought money passed hands as he spoke to the driver, then Lucien handed her in. They proceeded at a slow, steady pace along the streets. Though one or two other tourists shouted at their driver, he paid no attention, and they retained sole possession of the open vehicle with its hard leather seats and swaying, fringed top.

The driver, his flower-decked hat exactly matching the one on the head of his horse, began a running commentary on the points of interest they passed, until Lucien corrected him for the third time. Flinging a grin and a quick French phrase back at them, which made Lucien smile, he fell silent.

Even as Sherry watched the byplay, a part of her mind was busy with an odd discovery. Paul was not the only Villeré brother who possessed charm. For an instant she had glimpsed a hint of laughter in Lucien's black eyes. It had lightened the somber cast of his face and given him a startling attraction. A moment later, it was gone.

"What did he say?" Sherry asked, willing to be amused.

"Are you certain you want to know?"

"Yes, of course."

"He said he would leave me to show off in front of my woman, that he did not blame me for wanting to win your admiration."

Sherry gave him a cool stare, though she could not control the swift rise of color in her cheeks. "I don't see anything funny in that."

"No, you wouldn't," he answered, staring down at her with a peculiar expression at the back of his eyes. At that moment, the carriage rounded a corner. Sherry swayed on the seat, her bare forearm brushing the sleeve of his dinner jacket. A tiny shiver she could not suppress ran along her nerves and she drew away as if she had been stung. Although she directed her gaze elsewhere, pretending an intense interest in an ornate wrought-iron balcony, she was uncomfortably aware of the man at her side, and of the stern, unsmiling set of his mouth as he regarded her averted face.

The area around Jackson Square had been closed off to traffic, making a pedestrian mall of the brick streets. They alighted from their carriage near one of the barricades, and strolled into the enclosure.

Jackson Square faced the high levee of the Mississippi. Directly opposite the levee, with their backs turned to the rest of the Quarter, was the St. Louis Cathedral, and on either side, the Presbytere and the old Spanish government building called the Cabildo. Flanking these massive structures at right angles, forming the other two sides of the square, was the Pontalba buildings, erected in 1851 by Baroness Pontalba as the first apartment buildings in the New World. In the center of this square was the garden area surrounded by a tall black iron fence where stood the famous bronze statue of General Andrew Jackson, defender of New Orleans in the War of 1812.

At this time of day the area was nearly

deserted. The artists who hung their paintings on the cast-iron fence had packed up their canvases and gone home. The tourists had returned to their hotels to rest and contemplate their evening meal. The ice cream and popsicle wagons had called it a day, while the vendors of pralines and hot dogs had moved further over, to the vicinity of Bourbon Street. The lavender shadows of the soft Southern twilight were left to the iridescent gray pigeons that waddled here and there along the walks, and to the man and woman who stirred them into flight.

Sherry stood in the center of the fenced enclosure and stared around her. The ancient gray spire of the St. Louis Cathedral jousted with the clouds. Beneath the arches on the lower floor of the massive stone Cabildo and Presbytere glowed the orange fire of lighted lanterns. The Pontalba buildings stretched in graceful symmetry on either side, their slender, elegant columns, gables, and chimneys speaking of times past, and their weathered red brick taking on a soft radiance in the afterglow. Nearer to hand, the light breeze rustled in the head-high oleanders and bamboo cane. Water trickled in an antique fountain close by, and the statue of General Jackson, green with verdigris, reared against the sky. Forgetful of the identity of Lucien Villeré and of the part she was playing, Sherry turned to him to share her wonder and enjoyment with a smile. He was watching her, the expression in his eyes so cynical that her pleasure vanished. She found herself wishing fervently that she could explore the city alone.

Leaving the garden enclosure by the front gate, they walked along in front of the Presbytere and the Cathedral. Lucien, his tone masking polite boredom, explained the museums and exhibits housed in the collection of old buildings around them. They turned down a dim alley between the Cathedral and the Cabildo.

"This short cut is known as Pirate's Alley," Lucien said. "Don't ask me why. I don't know, unless it was because usually the area was quiet and deserted, a good place for muggings, two hundred years ago. The paving stones you are walking on came to New Orleans as ship ballast, since there is no natural rock in the alluvial soil of this part of Louisiana. Every bit of paving in the early days had to be imported. There on your right, directly behind the Cathedral, is St. Anthony's Garden. Before the Civil War, the garden was a favorite dueling ground."

"A dueling ground, behind a church?"

Sherry asked, glancing at the fence-enclosed garden with its shrubbery and old trees.

Lucien inclined his head without looking at her. "It was convenient to the old quadroon ballroom directly across the street, over there where that hotel stands now."

"You did say quadroon?"

"The practice of keeping a mistress is of long standing among the young men of the city. Before the Civil War, the woman was sometimes white, but more often a quadroon, a girl of mixed white and mulatto blood. Quadroon balls were arranged so that the women could be presented for the selection of white men of means and social standing. Under the circumstances, it was not unusual for tempers to flare. The slightest insult could result in a challenge, and the usual method of deciding which of two men could have a particularly beautiful girl was by trial of arms, swords and pistols on the field of honor."

"You sound as if you regret the passing of those days," Sherry said, slanting him a glance from the corner of her eye.

"Do I? I admit the method has a certain attractive simplicity."

"It seems to me, that in the case of two men disagreeing over one woman, it would have been fairer to allow the woman to choose which of the two men she preferred."

"Possibly, but then the prize would have gone to the man with the more money, and where is the fairness in that?"

"I doubt money would have been the most important object every time, but it seems no more unfair to me than allowing strength or skill with weapons to become the deciding factor."

"Granted, but the Code Duello also permitted room for courage and daring to play a part."

Once more, Sherry was reminded of the blood of pirates which ran in this man's veins. Her lips twitched in a sudden smile. "Oh well," she conceded. "I suppose there would have been few women able to resist that combination, especially in a man who was willing to risk his life for her."

He made no reply, leaving Sherry with the disconcerting feeling that she had somehow missed a point but had scored one as well. Did the man still think, despite Paul's claiming her as his fiancée, that her relationship with his brother was considerably closer than she would admit, that of his mistress, in fact? Did his mention of duels over such women in the past have some purpose? If so, she could not see it.

Antoine's Restaurant was neither large nor impressive, though the long line of people waiting outside on the uneven sidewalk was an indication of its lasting popularity. The bow-shaped front, with its triple mahogany doors, might have been confusing if it had not been for Lucien, who unhesitatingly chose the correct entrance. He was recognized at once, and whisked through the vestibule and main restaurant area to a smaller, less crowded dining room. Like the main area, this room was lined with mirrors to make it appear larger. There were ceiling fans overhead, and bentwood hat and coat racks beside the doors. With the black and white marble squares, the atmosphere was one of cleanliness and a Victorian dedication to the pleasures of fine dining.

Without consulting Sherry, Lucien ordered glasses of dry wine as an apéritif, and they sat sipping these while studying the menu. Since they were printed in French, Sherry allowed Lucien to order for her while she amused herself by watching their black clad waiter memorize every detail of the long list of dishes without recourse to pad or pencil. When he went away, she sat back, watching the people around her. Some were obviously tourists, but others were just as plainly Creole French residents.

Lucien leaned back in his chair and took up his wineglass, staring with moody intentness at the golden liquid it contained. "Sherry," he said, flicking a sudden upward glance in her direction. "Is that your real name?"

"It is," she replied, nettled by his tone that was shaded with disbelief.

"There is nothing wrong with assuming another name for the purpose of a career," he said, running his eyes over her honeycolored hair and slender figure. "As a model, for instance."

She gave him a direct look. "If you are inquiring as to my work experience, it should be easy enough for you to discover how long I have worked for the Villeré Shipping Lines. I took a secretarial course directly out of high school, and the job with the branch of your firm was my first. That accounts for my twenty-one-odd years. If you had wanted the story of my life, I am certain Paul could have told you."

"To be perfectly frank, Paul refuses to discuss you except in the most glowing of complimentary terms. The only time I remember Paul ever mentioning you, before this past weekend, was as an exceptionally beautiful girl he had met with an unusual name which had the sound of one of our endearments.

You may know of it, *Chérie*... dearest?"

"Paul explained it to me," she said. Aware of a faint warmth creeping to her hairline, she hurried on. "But surely he told you about our engagement?"

"No more than he said the other night over the phone."

"Don't you think he might have had more to say if you hadn't sent him out of town?" Sherry asked.

He did not answer, though his heavily lashed eyes hardened as his gaze rested on her slim fingers clasping her wineglass. It was a moment before Sherry realized what had drawn his attention. He was searching for a ring, some positive proof to support the relationship she claimed between his brother and herself.

She should have worn the betrothal ring, Sherry knew that. Of course, she could draw it from her bodice and place it on her finger before him, but some stubborn impulse prevented her. If he would not believe her given word, why should she demean herself by trying to convince him?

"How long have you known Paul?" Lucien asked abruptly.

"For the better part of a year."

"Nevertheless, this — engagement seems

56

rather sudden to me."

"It may have been a bit rushed," she conceded gently "because of the circumstances, but I feel sure the idea was in the back of Paul's mind all along."

His mouth tightened, a sign that she had scored a point. "Doesn't it trouble you that my brother was not free from a past engagement?"

"Oh, come — you can't be serious," she said, affecting a light laugh. "The way I understand it, that was only a case of puppy love, over long ago. Surely no one expects Paul to stand by something he may have said when he was a teen-ager. It isn't reasonable."

"No, not strictly speaking," Lucien answered. "Paul did commit himself at the time however, and to a young girl of good family. You may consider my attitude outdated, but I believe he has a responsibility to be certain he is free before he becomes involved with another woman. Paul has not been overly nice in his relationships in the last few years, but this is one time when I intend to see that he does the right thing."

This was so nearly in line with her own thinking that Sherry could not argue with it. She was saved from the necessity by the arrival of the waiter with their meal. The reference to herself as a woman with whom Paul had become involved, while Aimee was a young girl of good family, did not pass unnoticed. Though she flicked him an angry look across the table as her plate was placed in front of her, it was impossible to object.

They began their meal with shrimp, plump, pink and firm, on a bed of lettuce topped by a sauce flavored with tomato and a dash of horseradish. This was followed by pompano en papillote, a dish for which Antoine's was famous, made of pompano baked in a white sauce containing shrimp and crab inside an oiled paper bag. The recipe had originally been concocted by one of the restaurant's most famous chefs in honor of the first balloon ascension in New Orleans. With this went asparagus in butter and soufflé potatoes, the latter also a specialty of the house, uniform strips of white potato fried in oil of different temperatures so that they puffed up to a delicious golden lightness.

As one perfectly seasoned dish followed another, Sherry found her appetite equal to the occasion. Her feeling of constraint faded as she savored every bite. Once as she looked up, she found Lucien's eyes upon her with something like puzzlement in their depths.

Catching her gaze, he said, "Well, and does

Antoine's live up to your expectations?"

Sherry looked around her, unable to subdue her instinctive smile of pleasure and appreciation. "Yes," she said, "it does."

At that moment the lights suddenly dimmed to darkness. The diners immediately stopped eating and began to look around them.

"Don't worry," Lucien said. "It isn't a black-out, only a little extra entertainment."

Before he had finished speaking, Sherry saw dancing blue flames coming toward them. A waiter bearing a serving tray advanced into the room, stopping beside a table in the near corner. He placed his flaming dish on a serving table set up by a second waiter following behind him. Then, with a flourish, he began to stir the mixture in his dish. The blue flames with orange points leaped higher. At precisely the correct moment, the fire was smothered and the contents was ladled out on serving plates.

Flaming crepes suzette, thin pancakes filled with an orange sauce and then flambéd in brandy. Sherry had seen them served before, but never with quite such drama. When the lights came up, she found Lucien studying her once more.

"Would you like a flaming dessert?" he asked, though Sherry had the impression the suggestion was made at random, without reference to his true thoughts.

"I would like it," she confessed with a rueful smile, "but I couldn't possibly find room."

"We will finish our wine then and go. There is still much of the Vieux Carré you have not seen."

Lucien had ordered a bottle of white wine with their meal. It seemed that every time Sherry had sipped from her glass the waiter had appeared to raise the level to full once more. It was still brimming. She was not used to wine with her meals. All too aware of the warm glide of the pale liquid in her veins, she would have preferred to leave it, and would have if it had not been for the hint of challenge in the dark eyes of the man across the table.

Abruptly his gaze moved past her shoulder. He seemed to stiffen, then he was smiling, reaching for his wineglass. His dark gaze compelling as he stared into her sea-blue eyes, he leaned to touch the rim of his glass to hers in a gesture of silent intimacy.

Sherry blinked at the sudden warmth of his manner, returning the salute with a shade of awkwardness. She had just touched the wine in her glass to her lips when a man spoke behind her.

"Lucien! We haven't seen you in months. Where have you been hiding yourself?"

Lucien Villeré rose to shake hands with a man a bit shorter and older than himself but with the same general build and coloring. There was a similarity about their faces that told Sherry plainly that they were related. Beside the man stood a woman, obviously his wife and one of the family from the fond smile she leveled at Lucien and from her familiar, relaxed manner.

"Étienne, so nice to see you again. And you also, Estelle. May I present you to *ma Chérie?* Don't frown, Estelle, that is her name, Sherry." The introduction was made with a caressing smile that startled Sherry so she very nearly missed the offhand way in which she was dimissed with only her given name. Perhaps she would have overlooked it anyway if it had not been for the subtle alteration of the other woman's face and the abrupt withdrawal of her attention. Then color surged to Sherry's hairline as she realized that Lucien Villeré had deliberately avoided introducing her as Paul's fiancée, leading his relatives to the conclusion that she was little more than a playmate, and one of his at that!

Short of forcing her way into the conversation, there was nothing Sherry could do to correct the wrong impression. She hated scenes and loud voices, moreover, there was in the back of her mind a niggling suspicion that she might have contributed to the situation. She was not precisely dressed like a debutante. She contented herself with sending Lucien a look of smouldering dislike. For the first time, she allowed herself to look forward to appearing in public as Paul's fiancée. After this, the announcement of the engagement would make Lucien appear either a fool or an ill-mannered boor.

The woman called Estelle touched her husband on the arm, flicking an uneasy smile in Sherry's direction. At once, her husband began to ease out of the situation.

"Nice to run into you like this, Lucien. We don't get to see you often enough. I understand there is to be a party for the little Dubois girl a week from tonight. I expect we will see you there."

"Yes, of course," Lucien said. He took his seat once more as with a nod and a smile in Sherry's general direction, the couple moved away.

Sherry pushed her wineglass back. Taking up her napkin, she touched it to her lips. Most of the red lip gel she had used came away upon the linen cloth, but she hardly noticed. Placing the stained napkin beside her plate, she said, "They seemed like nice people, your relatives. It should be interesting to get to know them better."

Lucien sent her a sharp glance, as if surprised at her quiet irony, but did not answer. He drained his wine and set the glass aside. "Shall we go?" he asked, and at her nod, signaled for the check.

3

They strolled in the warm, somnolent night air once more. Lucien offered to drive her about the city, mentioning the Garden District and the Superdome as points of interest, but Sherry declined. She was in no hurry. There was no need to see everything in one day. Besides, the evening had not been so enjoyable that she wished to prolong it.

Lucien seemed in no hurry to return her to her hotel, however. He turned his footsteps in the opposite direction. In preoccupied silence they made their way down a street lined with antique shops. Drawn by the sound of music, they wandered into a lounge with its doors thrown wide. The band was playing Dixieland jazz, the mellow, melodious tunes blending perfectly with the night and the atmosphere. Where else but in New Orleans could it sound so right? Under its nostalgic spell, Sherry could not stay angry. It was a relief however that the volume of the music in that small room prevented Lucien and herself from exchanging anything more than a casual comment or two. It struck her once that Lucien was extremely abstracted, but she put it down to his familiarity with the type of entertainment she was enjoying.

When they left at last, the evening was advanced and the crowds on the streets beginning to thin.

"There is one more stop we must make," Lucien said, before they had gone more than a block.

"Oh?"

"The Café du Monde, near the French Market. It is a tradition here to finish off an evening with café au lait there. In truth, the tradition is to have an early breakfast at one of the coffee houses catering to the farmers who display their wares in the French Market before wending your way home after staying out all night, during Mardi Gras for instance, but I believe we can stretch a point."

Overcoming an odd reluctance, Sherry agreed. Café au lait, coffee with milk, sounded like a good way to round off the evening. Afterward, she would say goodnight and hope that for the rest of the week she would have Paul's support when she was in his brother's company.

The Café du Monde was only a few steps from Jackson Square and no more than a few yards from the Mississippi, separated from the water by a high, screening wall. Along the wall had been built a scenic walkway which overlooked the river, a part of the program to renovate and preserve the character of the French Quarter. Promenading on the levee, as Lucien explained while they waited for service, was also an old New Orleans custom.

The coffee was hot, strong, and rich with cream. Since she had had no dessert with dinner, Sherry was persuaded to accept an order of beignets, the crisp, golden fried French doughnuts drenched with powdered sugar for which the coffee houses were famous. The pastries, though delicious, were impossible to eat with dignity. Watching Lucien trying to keep the drifting white sugar from his black dinner jacket brought a smile to Sherry's mouth, one he answered with a rueful shake of his head. The plentiful paper napkins took the last of the gel from Sherry's lips, even as their roughness made her wince.

As Lucien raised a brow in inquiry, she touched the back of one hand to her cheek.

66

"Sunburn," she said, and met his sudden frown with an expression clear and questioning.

Lucien set his heavy coffee cup into its saucer and leaned back. "Tell me, Miss Mason," he said deliberately. "Are you in love with my brother?"

She looked up, caught off guard. "Why else would I marry him?"

"I can think of several reasons – money, position, maybe an idea of joining him in a round of the international playgrounds."

"What a strain it must be keeping up such a cynical attitude," she murmured.

"Call it a necessary means of protection."

"Protection? Against what, or whom, assuming you are speaking of yourself."

"Despite your efforts to change the subject, we were speaking of you."

"Were we? What I feel for Paul is not a matter for discussion with anyone except the man I am to marry," she told him, her turquoise eyes darkening with anger and something more, a weary distaste for the necessity of evasion.

"What of money? Is that subject also off limits except with Paul? Has he told you, for instance, that though he has part ownership in the Villeré Shipping Lines, his income is derived solely from his salary as an employee of the company?"

"No, he has not," she answered, her voice cold. "But it would make little difference. What I feel for Paul would be the same whether he was penniless or a millionaire." She could make that statement without a qualm. The sisterly affection she felt for the younger Villeré brother could not be affected by money or the lack of it.

Lucien stared at her. "I am almost inclined to believe you mean that," he said, a frown drawing his brows together. "But are you certain Paul feels as strongly about you?"

"I think he does."

"But you aren't sure? Has it occurred to you that your attachment to him is very useful to him at this time?"

She gave him a hard look. "I don't believe you know your brother very well if you are suggesting that he would pretend to love me merely to cut his ties with another woman. In any case, what would he gain? He would only have another entanglement to get out of." Paul might have mentioned some such scheme as Lucien had in mind, but it had been a wry joke, nothing more.

"If the end result were to persuade you to meet him in New Orleans for a few weeks, that might be gain enough."

"You—" Sherry began, then stopped. Hot words of defense for Paul and herself hovered on the tip of her tongue, along with a round condemnation of the type of interference in other people's lives which had driven Paul to this underhanded subterfuge. She would have given anything not to be involved, to be free to tell Lucien Villeré exactly what she thought. She could not. The best thing to do then was to get away from him before she said something she would regret.

Jumping to her feet, she slipped quickly between the crowded tables and made her way out of the café. The walkway along the river levee loomed before her and she took it, drawing her blouse higher and wrapping her shawl about her against a chill of the spirit and the cool night wind off the water. She scarcely glanced at the wide, sweeping curve of the Mississippi or the glittering points of light on the far shore. Her mind seethed with indignation and a bitter remorse that she had ever gotten herself into this fix. The moment she saw Paul she would tell him she wanted out of it. He would have to muddle through the best he could, even though she would hate giving Lucien Villeré the satisfaction of thinking he had scared her away.

The sound of footsteps alerted her to Lucien's slow approach. Since she had no desire to have him chasing after her or following like a shadow while she walked back to the hotel, she came to a halt. She leaned her forearms on the balustrade, her face averted.

He stopped beside her, a tall, faintly threatening presence in the darkness lit only by distant mercury vapor street lamps. For long moments silence stretched between them. At last he spoke.

"Sherry — *Chérie*—"

She turned, her deep blue eyes wide with surprise at the soft, almost tentative sound of her name on his lips.

He stared down at her, his gaze moving over the blowing tendrils of soft hair about her face, the guileless depths of her eyes, the pure lines of her mouth, without its coating of color. With her neckline drawn high and the light material of her dress fluttering around her, she had a look of unconscious vulnerability.

He shook his head as though to clear it. "If you are determined to go through with this, determined to see Paul," he said, his voice harsh, "I can take you to him."

"I — I thought you said he was out of town?"

"He is. I have a place on the bayous that I use for a fishing and hunting camp and a retreat. I sent him out there to entertain a business client who was in town for a few days. I am certain I would have had more trouble persuading him to go if he had known you were coming today. Unfortunately, he didn't know. His secretary, as a matter of procedure, verified the making of your plane and hotel reservations through my office, and I instructed my secretary to handle the arrangements."

She turned her gaze, cold with contempt for his high-handed interference, full upon him. The limousine, the expensive hotel. She should have guessed something was wrong. "I will pay you back, every cent. I told Paul I would rather make my own arrangements."

"It doesn't matter — now. Do you want to go out to the camp or would you prefer to wait until Paul returns?"

Sherry pressed her lips together. Despite Lucien's high-handed methods, the offer to take her to Paul was a concession. In some way she must have convinced him of her sincerity. She could not afford to stay at the hotel Lucien had chosen. Paul had mentioned this fishing camp, Lucien's retreat, a number of times. It was a large place, from all accounts, a modernized plantation house. She should not be too much in the way, even if there were business clients around. Anyway, she would not be staying long. The sooner she saw Paul, the sooner this masquerade would be over. "I would like to go, if it isn't too much trouble."

"Not at all," he replied, his tone carefully neutral. "We can reach there before dawn. Tomorrow is Sunday so there will be no hurry about returning."

"You mean — leave tonight?"

"It would be best, if you are determined to see him."

There was an undercurrent in his voice which sent a tremor along her nerves. She slanted a glance at him in the dimness, seeing the chiseled planes of his bronze face, the firm lines of his lips and his dark, unreadable eyes. There was something taut in his stance that communicated itself to her, as though he attached unusual importance to her answer.

"Tonight it is then," she said, but found she could not respond to his sudden, tight smile.

The cabin cruiser was blue and white with sleek, rakish lines and brass work that gleamed in the glow of the running lights. It sliced effortlessly through the muddy water, heading into the dark night. Its powerful motor throbbed in the paneled cabin below decks where Sherry lay. It would be a trip of several hours to the fishing camp; it had seemed wise to follow Lucien's suggestion that she rest. But whether it was the swish and swirl of the water along the hull of the boat, or the knowledge that she was alone upon it with a man she hardly knew, she lay wide awake with her arms crossed behind her head, staring up at the ceiling. In spite of the fact that the bunk built against the wall to conserve space in the nicely appointed cabin was extremely comfortable, she could not sleep.

Was this a foolish thing she was doing? Somehow Lucien's about-face filled her with a growing feeling of disquiet. It was not in character for him to give way to a woman, she thought, and she could not feel that her determined stand against him, or her meager explanations of her relationship with Paul, had been sufficient to make him change his mind. It could be he had had a sudden urge to see what the effect of her sudden appearance would be on his brother. One thing she was convinced of – this trip was no mere whim, no easy acquiescence. There had to be a reason.

As certainty grew, so did her unease, and

she wished she had not been so quick to accept Lucien Villeré's offer. But with their hurried return to the hotel so that she could pack her things, there had been no time to consider the reasons behind it. Now, in retrospect, she had the feeling that she had been rushed. And she did not like that feeling.

Sherry stared up into the dark ceiling until her eyes burned. The more she thought of Lucien's interference, the more unbelievable it seemed. She had heard of the old French tradition of the authority of the head of the family, still she had never thought to see it in action. She was happy she did not have to endure it. She was also surprised that Paul would. Was he, perhaps, more immature than she had realized, and Lucien felt he was responsible for straightening out his affairs?

Affairs. An unfortunate choice of words. She was not having an affair with Paul, though she was sure nothing she could say would convince Lucien otherwise. That fact had been made plain enough by the way he had failed to introduce her to his relatives in the restaurant. Now, when it was too late, she regretted the angry impulse which had caused her to defy his wrong impression of her. She should have faced him as a quiet, demure young thing, a victim of Paul's fatal charm and his carelessness with the affections of young women. Lucien would have been in a real quandary then, forced to decide which of the two, Aimee or herself, Paul had wronged more.

Under the circumstances, she supposed she should be glad that she had not been packed ignominiously off to the airport and put on the first flight back to St. Louis. Short of throwing her job in Lucien's face, there would have been little she could have done about it. That he had relented enough to take her to Paul should be a reason for satisfaction, and would be, if she did not have this uncomfortable feeling that his reasons for it were strictly his own.

What would Paul say when he learned that Lucien had intercepted her arrival? Would he laugh it off, or would he be idignant for her sake? She was by no means certain her supposed fiancée dared to clash head-on with his formidable elder brother. If he had, he would have done so over the question of his long-time commitment to Aimee. There would have been no hurried flight to St. Louis. He would never have made a midnight visit to her apartment. And she would not be here, lying in sleepless apprehension, aboard a boat in the Mississippi channel below New Orleans with a man she had known less than twenty-four hours.

The river tonight was just as dangerous, just as filled with snags and floating debris and shifting sandbars as it had ever been in the days of the steamboats. The safety of the boat and herself depended on Lucien Villeré's knowledge of the river and his quick reflexes. Physical safety was not what concerned her, however.

With an exclamation of impatience she swung her legs off the bunk and reached above her to switch on the light. Rummaging in her suitcase, she found her jeans and a long-sleeved shirt. They would be more suitable than the evening gown she had taken off to save it from wrinkling while she lay down. Though she had not packed a sweater, she could have used one against the damp night air. It was surprisingly cool on the river.

She had taken her hair down before she crawled into the bunk. Now she tied a length of ribbon around it to keep it out of her face, leaving the ends streaming down her back. A wry grin curved her mouth. If she had gone about it deliberately she could not have done a better job of turning herself into a country girl, the antithesis of the kind of woman Lucien considered her to be. Would he notice? She doubted it very much.

Slipping into canvas shoes, she made her way cautiously, watching for the rock of sudden waves, from the sleeping area back to a tiny compact galley. It contained a minute sink of gleaming stainless steel and a small but serviceable built-in gas range. In the neat cabinets she discovered what she had been searching for — a kettle, a coffeepot, and a container of coffee. Filling the kettle, she set it on the gas burner, a faint frown between her brows. Lucien might find a cup of coffee agreeable too. There was no harm in making the offer. Open antagonism would get them nowhere. Now that she had gained a certain measure of acceptance, it was pointless to harbor a grudge.

She found a rattan tray, then hunted out cups and saucers, sugar packets, and a jar of instant creamer. As she stood leaning against the back of the eating booth, waiting for the water to boil, she heard a change in the cruiser's motors. An instant later they ground to a halt. Pushing aside the curtains that covered the porthole, Sherry cupped her hands around her eyes and peered through the glass.

She could see very little in the darkness; still it seemed that the boat was in a lock of some sort. Were they leaving the river, then? It appeared so.

Just then the kettle began to whistle and she turned to pour the coffee water into the pot. By the time the brew had dripped they were again on their way, though she felt they were not moving quite so swiftly as before.

With a glance around to be sure she had left the galley as tidy as she had found it, she carried the tray with the filled cups and cream and sugar up the steep steps to the deck, ducking as she eased out the small door. Lucien stood before the wheel.

"Coffee?" she said with a forced brightness as she stopped beside him.

He barely glanced at her. "What are you doing up?"

"Too keyed-up to sleep." Since he had not refused the coffee, she set his cup off onto the instrument console within easy reach. "Cream and sugar?"

He shook his head without taking his eyes from the twisting stream beyond the windscreen.

The strong searchlight mounted on the roof of the cabin cruiser bored a tunnel into the darkness. It illuminated the gray-green banks of the stream they were navigating, now and then picking out the gleaming red and green eyes of startled night creatures. The sound of their engines vibrated around them, echoing back from the close-pressing swampland.

Sherry slanted a glance at the man beside her. He had taken a few minutes, after coming aboard, to exchange his evening jacket, shirt, and tie for a dark knit shirt, and his leather shoes for canvas loafers that would grip the deck. His hands held the wheel with an easy competence, and yet his face, in the dim light of the instrument panel, was set in the same harsh lines as earlier. His eyes were narrowed in concentration and there was a determined thrust to his chin. Sherry thought, however, that the job at hand, the piloting of the boat along this narrow body of water, did not have his whole attention. On the other hand, she could not convince herself that it was she who occupied his thoughts. It was more as if he had a problem on his mind, something that he had no intention of leaving unsettled.

She took up her own cup and raised it to her lips. More for something to say than from any wish for the information, she asked, "Is it much further?"

"To Bayou's End? Depends on your definition of far," he answered noncommittally.

"From what Paul has told me of it, it sounds like a great place to get away from it all."

79

"I've never known Paul to need to get away, but yes, I'd say it serves that purpose well." Without urging, he went on. "It was once a sugar plantation, built by my great-great-grandfather. He was a sea captain and liked the easy access to the gulf through the bayous. It was a profitable venture for nearly a hundred years, until storms from the gulf several years in succession covered the land with salt water. The house stood empty for a time, then some fifteen years ago it was renovated for use as a vacation and weekend cottage."

"I thought you called it a hunting and fishing camp earlier."

"Camp is a local term for a vacation home. As for hunting and fishing, we are in the path of the great southeastern flyway for the annual bird migrations. We get duck and geese as well as the more decorative species. The freshwater fishing is good, of course. And, as I said, it's not so far from the gulf by the back door, the bayous. We go out often for tarpon and red snapper or pompano."

"Does Paul go to — to Bayou's End often?"

He shook his head, smiling without amusement. "Not often, and then it's usually with a crowd. There are a few uncles, cousins, friends, and men from the office that come down during the hunting and fishing seasons in a party. Paul plays host then, as a rule."

"I can imagine." Sherry smiled, thinking of Paul and his liking for people, for gaiety and good times. She felt rather than saw Lucien's quick look at her. She thought he was going to comment, but the impulse was obviously quelled.

Such indecision was unlike him, she felt, and she found herself turning over in her mind the possible comments he might have made. Was he going to tell her it was not only men whom Paul had invited to Bayou's End? Why had he stopped? The fact would hardly be a surprise. Paul had never made a secret of his pleasure in the company of women. It was a part of his charm that he liked and appreciated her sex. So many men gave the impression of seeking the company of women for one purpose only and that against their finer instincts. They had little use for women as companions, and nothing but amused contempt for their conversation and their thought processes. Paul, without departing in the least from his masculine point of view, seemed to find everything about them enjoyable and interesting.

The silence between them spread until she was aware of the sound of the insects and the chorus of the frogs above the hum of the outboard motors, the evidence of teeming life beyond their light beam.

"I appreciate your going to so much trouble to take me to Paul," Sherry said after a moment. "I hadn't realized it would be quite so far, or I would have tried to make other arrangements."

"Not at all, *Chérie,*" he returned. "I am only too happy to take you to Bayou's End. Besides, I expect you would have had difficulties getting there alone. There are no regular means of transportation to the camp. You would have had to hire a boat, and even if you had found someone willing, there is no guarantee that they would have been able to find the place."

"Not able to find it? Is it so remote then?"

"Remote, yes. But there is also the nature of the bayou country to consider. The streams twist and turn for hundreds of miles, one leading into the other, sometimes dividing a dozen times in a mile stretch. The direction they run is not always the same; it depends on the weather, the tides, the time of year. Sometimes they don't run at all. Some are so wide that it is impossible to identify a friend on the opposite bank, while others are so narrow that it's possible to touch the sides with your outstretched hands. A few are deep, but others are so shallow that they amount to little more than dew over mud. Some bayous head for the gulf with no nonsense, others meander for miles, then suddenly disappear. Even men born and raised on the bayou can get lost, especially during flood times or bad weather. There are few landmarks, and the oaks, the cypress, the Spanish moss, the alligator grass, and water hyacinths have a sameness about them."

"I – see. Then I am even more in your debt, Mr. Villeré."

"Call me Lucien," he said with a strange smile and a Gallic flick of the fingers that made nothing of her gratitude. But though Sherry had thought of him by his first name in her mind, she did not avail herself of his permission to use it. There was a strange sort of intimacy in their being alone on the boat at night in the loneliness of the encroaching bayou country. She saw no reason to add to it.

And yet, for all her caution, her next words, coming almost without volition, were personal.

"You aren't married, are you?"

Lucien looked at her. "No."

"I thought not," she said, aware of the heated rise of blood to her face.

"Would you care to explain?"

She shook her head. "I was only going by

something I heard Paul say, plus the fact that you set off tonight without telling anyone where you were going." He had also been willing to allow his relatives, Étienne and Estelle, to consider her his mistress, scarcely the act of a married man, though she had no intention of trying to explain that bit of reasoning.

"Does it matter?" he asked, slanting her a quick glance.

Since she had embarked on this line of conversation, she might as well see it to the end. "Not particularly," she answered. "It just seemed strange to me that you, who have managed to shy away from the altar all these years, should take such an interest in the girl your brother marries. If it makes such a difference whom you welcome into the Villeré family, surely the least you could do is set him a good example."

"Isn't that a poor reason for tying myself to someone for life?"

"There are all the usual reasons, of course — a home, a family, to perpetuate an aristocracy of French Creole merchant princes."

"Is that how you think of me?" he queried, a hard edge to his tone. "Cold-blooded and calculating? I will have to see what can be done to change your mind."

4

Ahead of them the bayou forked and unhesitatingly Lucien swerved to the left. Seizing on this action as a change of subject and a means of breaking the peculiar tension between them, Sherry asked, "How do you find your way through the bayous if they are so dangerous?"

"Practice, Sherry. You need not be nervous. I have been taking this route for twenty years, since I was a boy of twelve."

Lucien reached out and picked up his mug. When he spoke again his voice was bland.

"You make a good cup of coffee."

"Thank you," she said without looking at him.

"You are also a beautiful young woman, but I'm sure you are aware of that."

Sherry flicked him a suspicious glance

through her lashes but made no reply.

"Intelligent, also," he went on. "Intelligent enough to know that the simple approach is best in my case." He eyed her jeans and she flushed, aware of her own thoughts on that score earlier.

"Look, Mr. Villeré—"

"I thought we had decided that I should be Lucien."

Her voice overrode his suggestion. "I did not dress for your benefit and you must admit that if I had wanted to it would be highly unlikely that I would just happen to have the necessary clothes with me."

A smile tugging at the corner of his mouth, he ignored her attempt at reasonableness. "Yes, I find a great deal to applaud in my brother's choice of an unofficial fiancée. His taste, it seems, is improving. I must not forget to tell him so."

"There is no need for this, I assure you," Sherry said, setting down her cup. "What I think of you, or, for that matter, what you think of me, makes no difference!"

"Doesn't it? I think you will find you are mistaken."

They were perilously close to an open rift. Afraid she would say something she would regret, Sherry whirled to go below.

Without letting go of the wheel, Lucien caught her arm. "Not leaving?" he asked. "Don't tell me you aren't enjoying my company. After all, it was you who sought me out."

"I did not!"

"Didn't you?"

"If you can't accept a friendly gesture like a cup of coffee—"

"Oh, but I can — when one is extended. I can also tell the difference between a friendly gesture and an attempt to influence me by the discreet application of sweet concern."

"Why, you conceited— Why should I exert myself that much? I don't need your support. I have Paul's!"

"Why so angry?" he asked. "I've admitted, haven't I, that I'm impressed. You have, in fact, my full attention."

It was true. As he spoke, Lucien had cut the motors. Their only movement was the drifting forward motion of their lost impetus.

Startled into silence, she stared up into his face. She did not like the suggestive tone in his voice, nor his closeness in the confines of the cockpit. The last thing she wanted was his full attention, not if he meant what she suspected. She recalled distinctly her misgivings about being alone with this man, a near-stranger, in such isolated surroundings at night. They returned a hundredfold as she thought of the unflattering opinion he held of her moral character and his ideas of the nature of her relationship with his brother.

Seeing the doubt mirrored in her eyes, a grim smile curved his mouth, widening until his white teeth gleamed in the tan of his face. His eyes were dark and magnetic, shielded by his thick lashes. The black shirt, molded to his broad chest, gave him a rakish look that had been lacking in more formal wear, the look of a corsair. All he needed was the golden gleam of an earring in his ear.

The sheer fancifulness of that fleeting observation, so unlike her usual well-ordered thoughts, startled Sherry so that she was able to catch at her dwindling self-possession. With deliberation, she looked around her at the enclosing night and the trees leaning to dip gray fingers of Spanish moss in the water ahead of them. Her voice laced with irony, she said, "Why are we stopping? Have you decided to live up to the reputation of your buccaneering ancestor?"

His face went blank, then laughter leaped into his eyes. "Paul told you about him, did he? Did he also tell you that he took a fair captive from one of the ships he boarded and sailed away with her to make her his bride?"

A frown flitted across Sherry's face, leaving her turquoise eyes troubled. "No, he never went into details."

"A pity. For a moment I thought you might have been put on your guard."

"On my guard? What do you mean?" She tilted her head to one side and her hair, shining like silk in the glow of the running lights, slid over her shoulder.

His eyes narrowed for an instant before he gave her an easy smile. "Against my piratical instincts of course," he said. "What else?"

What else indeed? And yet, for an instant Sherry had caught a glimpse of something hard and implacable in his manner. The touch of his fingers burned through the thin cotton of her shirtsleeve. Though his grasp was firm, it was not hurtful, still she was aware as she had never been before of the latent strength held in leash in a man's body.

Abruptly the boat, washed by the recoil of their own wake, scraped the bank. A tree limb scratched along the hull, coming to rest in a shower of dirt and debris against the windshield of the boat. Lucien released Sherry after a steadying moment. "You had better go below before you get a spider down your collar," he said.

It seemed like good advice. Sherry took it. It was not until she was lying once more in her bunk, staring into the darkness, that she allowed herself to savor her relief, and the feeling that somehow she had gained a reprieve.

A muffled thump followed by an unnatural quiet shook Sherry from sleep. She had not expected to close her eyes, but the quiet roar of the engines and the movement of the boat in the water, combined with her long and trying day, had lulled her to rest. Now the engines were silent, and the soft light of dawn filled the cabin. They had arrived at the place called Bayou's End.

The last thing she wanted was to be caught in bed. She jumped up at once. By the time the tap came on the cabin door she had washed her face, applied a hint of fresh makeup, and removed all evidence of her occupancy.

The first probing rays of the sun were just lighting the sky as she stepped from the boat to the weathered dock jutting out from the bank. They were tied at the edge of a wide body of water, like a small lake. A sloping emerald green lawn rose from the shoreline toward a large white house half-hidden among the trees.

Sherry looked around for some sign of Paul's presence. There was none. Two or three lightweight aluminum boats were pulled up on the bank, resting bottom-up. Beside them lay a small wooden craft which she took to be a pirogue. Since none of these could have transported Paul and his business client from New Orleans, she turned to Lucien with a question in her eyes.

Lucien, staring past her to where a black woman in a print dress and a starched white apron was coming toward them through the trees, appeared not to notice. He lifted his hand in greeting, his mouth relaxing in a smile.

"M'sieur Lucien! *Comment ça va?*" the woman called as she came nearer. Without giving him time to answer, she poured out a long, involved sentence in what had the sound of French patois. Lucien answered her in the same language before turning to Sherry.

"You mustn't feel slighted, *Chérie.* Marie doesn't have a word of English. She and her husband Jules have taken care of Bayou's End for us ever since they married, well before it became a fishing and hunting camp. Her people have been here for generations. Come, she will give us breakfast."

"But—Paul. Where is he?"

Lucien shrugged. "Out fishing maybe. We'll see." He indicated that she should precede him up the path toward the house standing at the top of the slight incline.

Live oaks hung with swags of gray Spanish moss, their ends flipping in the morning breeze, were dotted over the spreading lawn. When the house came into full view beyond them, Sherry's footsteps lagged while she stared. It was larger than she had pictured in her mind, more imposing than a weekend cottage had any right to be, despite the fact that it had once been a plantation home. Old it must be indeed, for it was built in the French West Indies planter's style that had predated the more common Greek Revival type by several decades. Raised on thick, square pillars for protection against floods, it boasted a tall flight of wide steps with outcurving banisters. The steep roof, hinting at high ceilings, sloped out to cover deep verandas, or galleries, on three sides. Beneath this shaded protection, rows of shuttered French windows indicated that each principal room opened to the outside for convenience and the free circulation of air. The front entrance, directly beyond the steps, featured a massive door topped by a beautiful old fanlight of leaded glass in the rising sun pattern, with sidelights of small, decorative glass panes.

From the top of the steps she looked back. Down the slope through the trees she could see the white cruiser tied to the small dock. The boat rode gently upon its pale reflection in the water. Beyond it was the still pool with cypress trees up to their knees in water, their outstretched branches clothed with fine cut foliage feathers of pale green.

"It's a beautiful place," she said. "More like a lake than a bayou."

"That's what it is. The bayou runs into this open place. There are several small runoffs, most too shallow to be navigated, that carry the overflow away down below us, but for all purposes this lake is where the bayou ends." He lifted a quizzical brow and she smiled slightly, acknowledging the allusion to the name of the house.

The water shone with a glassy sheen, like a dark mirror, lapping gently against the pilings of the dock. Near the shore was a patch of water hyacinths, the mauve flowers making a splotch of delicate color. Slowly a giant white crane lifted from his perch on a tree limb to fly away, the slow and stately precision of its wing beat lifting it above the trees. There was peacefulness in the scene, but there was also something else, a quality of waiting that disturbed her.

Breakfast was served on the front gallery, a light repast of hot, black coffee, fresh apple tarts, and a selection of fruit. Whether it was because of the early hour or an odd oppression of the spirit, Sherry found she was not hungry. She forced down a tart and drank her coffee in silence. Marie, hurrying back and forth between the table and a serving cart brought from the back regions of the house, talked volubly, but Sherry could not understand a word she was saying. Lucien, laughing and joking with the housekeeper, seemed to find no opportunity to ask the question that he knew very well burned in the forefront of her mind. Or if he did, he was in no hurry to translate the answer.

When Marie retreated finally to the rear of the house, Sherry directed a level look at Lucien. "Well?"

"Well what?" he asked, reaching with unimpaired appetite for a peach from the fruit bowl in the center of the table.

"Is Paul fishing?"

"Does it matter?"

"Of course it matters," she said, staring at him in perplexity. "If Paul isn't fishing, then he may not be here at all. And if he isn't, if he has already returned to New Orleans, then

I will have to go back with you."

For an instant he was still, then he picked up a knife and began to peel the peach. "Paul is not here. More than that, he has not been here and has no intention of coming."

Sherry stared at him. If something had happened to Paul, then his brother would not be calmly sitting, enjoying his breakfast. "Are — are you trying to say that you lied to me, that Paul never left New Orleans?"

"To the best of my knowledge, he is sound asleep at his French Quarter apartment."

"I suppose he was there all the time. That must have given you a few bad moments as we walked over the Quarter."

"Not at all, since I knew he was spending the afternoon and evening with Aimee at my mother's home on Lake Pontchartrain."

From the direction of the dock came a man toward them, no doubt Marie's husband, Jules. Under each arm he carried one of Sherry's suitcases. Sherry swallowed as the nerves tightened in her throat. She could feel the painful spread of apprehension as it raced with the blood along her veins. She rushed into speech, though she knew the words were foolish before they were out of her mouth.

"He's bringing my bags from the boat. Shouldn't you stop him?"

Lucien followed her gaze, but he made no move to halt Jules or to have her luggage returned.

"Lucien—" Sherry began, then stopped, all too aware of the strange, strained sound of his name on her lips.

"You will need your things," he said, his tone so flat and final that there could be no misunderstanding his meaning.

"How long are we staying?" she asked, her chin coming up.

"I am here for the day," he answered. "As for you, it depends."

"On?"

"On you."

"In what way?" she asked, her voice conveying no vestige of encouragement.

"You were right last night. Without intending to in the least, I have taken the same kind of action as my buccaneering ancestor. The difference is, I have no designs on you. My sole intention is to keep you here for a few days, until after the party for Aimee, a grace period wherein Paul and Aimee can get to know one another without interference or distraction."

"I don't understand why you've gone to such trouble. Why didn't you just refuse to make my traveling arrangements, even tell my boss in St. Louis to fire me?"

"And have you show up down here on your own, a martyr? That would have been the best possible way to ensure my brother's continued interest in you. In any case, I wanted to see for myself what you were like, to satisfy myself that Paul wasn't using you to get out of what he thought was going to be an unpleasant chore."

Sherry took a deep breath. "Suppose," she said carefully, "that I were to give you my word that I would return to St. Louis without communicating with Paul."

"You would do that? So much for the love match of the century then if you give up so easily. I never expected it."

The sarcasm in his voice reached Sherry like the flick of a whip. She would not tell him the real reason she was in New Orleans, however, though not entirely for Paul's sake. Now, at this moment, the subterfuge in which they were involved seemed so shoddy and stupid that she would have given much if she could have turned back time and refused to have anything to do with it.

"No answer?" Lucien inquired. "I wonder why. Did I touch a nerve, or are you waiting for me to be taken in by your sacrifice? Sorry, but I have no intention of letting you anywhere near a telephone, whether you give your word or not."

"Paul will have to know sometime what you've done."

"Agreed, but I will choose the time and the place. Until then you will stay here at Bayou's End."

She stared at him as the force of what he was saying swept in upon her. She thought of this isolated fishing and hunting camp to which she had been brought by waterways too intricate and too dangerous for her to find her way back alone, of the servants with whom she could not communicate, and who would probably retire at night to their own private bungalow. She had walked into his trap so trustingly, so blithely.

A rush of saving anger swept over her. "You can't do this!" she cried. "It's kidnapping, and there are laws against it!"

"Try convincing the police that I, Lucien Villeré, abducted you from your hotel room and dragged you, screaming of course, out of a crowded hotel lobby and onto my boat. Try it and I don't doubt that I can bring forth a dozen witnesses who will swear that you came of your own free will. As for these few days you will spend here at Bayou's End, if I explain that you accepted my invitation to spend them at my retreat there are few who would see any reason to doubt that you came with me, as the saying goes, with your eyes open."

"Are you trying to tell me that your position in New Orleans puts you above the law?" she demanded.

"Not quite," he said with maddening calm. "I believe my standing and reputation will survive any charges you may lay against me, however. What I am trying to tell you is this. The kind of freedom enjoyed by today's young women like you, who go where and with whom they please, has made it practically impossible for our over-worked police to protect their lives, much less their virtue."

The color slowly drained from her face as she realized that he was right. Who would believe it? She hardly believed it herself. She gripped her hands together, glancing up at him briefly through her eyelashes.

"Isn't this a great deal of trouble to go to keep Paul from seeing me, especially since you're so convinced I mean nothing to him?"

"Consider it a compliment," he answered. "If, after meeting you, I had not thought you were a definite threat to his engagement, I would not have bothered."

"I'm flattered," she said, an attempt at irony that did not quite come off.

He lounged back in his chair, a gleam of triumph lighting his eyes. He had won. He was a man who was used to forcing his will upon others and having them accept it without complaint. Because she did not scream with temper, because she sat quietly, he was certain that she too was going to accept his will without opposition. He was so positive of it that, when Marie came to the door and spoke to him, he rose without hesitation and went into the house with her, leaving Sherry alone on the gallery.

Sherry thought that she had caught Jules' name. Since he had passed them carrying her cases into the house, perhaps Marie wanted to know which room to allot to her. In that case, she would only have a moment.

Stealthily she left her chair and eased down the wide steps. The boat lay there before her, white and sleek in the sunlight. The bayous were confusing but she would take her chances. They could not be completely uninhabited. There must be people somewhere who could direct her back to the city. She would have to leave her clothes behind, but she could wire her bank for money once she was back in New Orleans. She was not used to having someone's will imposed upon her own in that high-handed fashion, and she did not intend to submit meekly!

As soon as the oak trees began to cover her escape from the view of the house, she ran. At the dock she paused to toss the mooring lines onto the deck of the boat. Then, with a light jump she landed beside them. In seconds she was slipping into the seat behind the instrument panel. The key hung in the ignition and, breathing a prayer of thanksgiving, she grasped it and gave it a turn. Nothing happened.

"Think," she chided herself. She could drive a car, why not a boat? She ran her eyes over the controls, the knobs and levers. What had Lucien done when he had restarted the engines a few hours ago, just before she had left him to go below? This lever? Yes, maybe. Once again she tried the key. Still nothing. Gears then. Where were they? She pushed another lever, tried again. Nothing. An adjustment, a faint sound, almost catching. With trembling fingers she adjusted the controls. Almost again. One more adjustment. Yes! The engines caught, roaring into life.

And now, gently, slowly, she pulled back on the throttle. The boat was moving!

A fierce exultation raced through her veins. The boat was moving! Let Lucien Villeré find his own way back to civilization. She hoped he had to paddle one of the aluminum boats until his arms fell out.

Behind her there was a shout. She heard the thud of footsteps on the dock and swung around in time to see Lucien make a flying leap to the deck of the boat. The trim craft rocked with the jar of his weight and Sherry clung to the wheel to steady it. An instant later a hand clamped down on her wrist with a firm grip. Strong arms encircled her and she was swept against a hard-muscled chest while the wheel of the cabin cruiser swung drunkenly.

She felt the vibration of Lucien's laugh as, taking advantage of her stiff reaction to his closeness, he leaned to switch off the ignition. He did it with such ease, such assurance, that rage boiled up inside her. Suddenly she kicked out at his shins, fighting him there in the drifting boat with every ounce of her strength, twisting, turning, pummeling, trying to claw in a primitive fury, uncaring of the pain she inflicted.

It was no good. She could not defeat his steely grasp. At last she lay in his arms with her bruised wrists behind her back. Her breath came in labored gasps and tears of hate and frustration stood in her turquoise eyes like the wash of a storm across a Southern sky.

As the resistance left her, Lucien's clasp loosened a fraction. He surveyed her flushed face, his gaze lingering on her parted lips. "I never meant to hurt you," he said quietly, "but I warn you. I meant every word I said. You will stay here with me until I say you can go."

Sherry took a deep, steadying breath. "Do you expect me to accept that? I can't. I won't. You may have won this time, but there will be others. I'm not beaten yet."

A flash of something like admiration shone briefly in his eyes before they narrowed. "No?" he queried. "Shall we see how far your defiance goes?"

She guessed his intent, but there was nothing she could do. A soft cry of protest rose to her lips as his mouth came down on hers. She closed her eyes, assailed by waves of sensation – disbelief, humiliation, helpless anger, and also the purely tactile feel of his arms holding her against him and his mouth on hers.

When he raised his head, he stared at her a long moment. Abruptly he released her, turning to the controls of the boat. As stiff and straight as any captive, she stood beside him, held by one wrist, as he maneuvered the cabin cruiser back to the dock.

Jules was waiting to fasten the mooring lines. Lucien took the keys from the ignition with deliberate slowness and pushed them into his pants pocket. Turning to her, he scooped her up into his arms. With effortless ease he leaped to the dock and strode with her back up the slope to the house.

Marie, standing in the doorway, called out something with a teasing light in her eyes and a warm laugh.

"Yes," Lucien replied before he said in English for Sherry's benefit, "She thinks we are having a lovers' quarrel, a small difference over the secluded nature of this place far away from the pleasures of the city."

"I wonder where she got that idea?" Sherry said through her teeth. Though she knew it would do no good, she appealed to the other woman. "It was no lovers' quarrel. I've been kidnapped, shanghaied, brought here against my will. I hate this man!"

The housekeeper only shook her head with a laughing comment. When Lucien translated, Sherry lapsed into hopeless silence. For the woman had said: "She has spirit, that one. But what good is a woman without it — especially to a man like M'sieur?"

He placed her in a rattan chair on the gallery then, and with a flamboyant gesture for the delectation of Marie and Jules, he pressed a kiss into the palm of her hand. From that vantage point she was forced to watch as Jules and Lucien, with wide grins, many comments, and much masculine laughter, pulled up the lightweight boats and fastened them with a stout chain to a solid oak tree, locking them in place. He was taking no chances, a fact that was brought home to her when he came to stand before her with his hands on his hips.

"I would advise against trying to swim for it," he said, his teeth flashing white in the tan of his face, "unless you have a liking for alligators and snakes."

"I think I would prefer their company to yours," she replied evenly.

"My feelings are hurt. However, I don't believe you would be so foolhardy as to put it to the test."

It was unanswerable, and as she sat there, caught in his mocking gaze, she despised him for that too.

5

It was Lucien who suggested, a short time later, that Marie show his guest to her room. The prospect was more than welcome. Sherry had been by no means certain she would not have to endure his constant company for the length of her stay. As she followed the house-keeper from the gallery she allowed herself to feel relief, and also a measure of satisfaction that Lucien was no more anxious to play the ever-watchful guard than she was to be guard-ed. An instant later she frowned. His dis-missal could also mean he saw no reason to stand watch since he was certain there was no escape.

The bedroom she had been given was large and airy with a high ceiling and tall French windows that opened out onto the gallery both on the front and the side. It had its own modern bath through a connecting door in what must once have been a dressing room. The furnishings included a tester bed, a great wardrobe known as an armoire, and a washstand complete with a Victorian marble top upon which sat an antique pitcher and bowl. The room, with its cream-colored crocheted spread, rose drapes and bed hangings, its cream, rose, and green Aubusson-style carpet, all in miracle fabrics, was a harmonious blend of old and new, charm and practicality.

When the door had closed behind Marie, Sherry dropped onto the edge of the bed. Staring at the floral pattern of the carpet, she shook her head. It was unbelievable. Despite everything, she could not rid herself of the feeling that this could not be happening. This was the twentieth century, for heaven's sake! No matter how much a man might dislike a situation, he did not react with such a drastic solution, did he?

Some did. Lucien Villeré, that hard, decisive businessman with his penchant for rapier tactics was one of them.

How had she got herself into this mess? It was no use blaming Paul. The idea might have been his, but she had gone into it of her own free will. There had been plenty of time to back out. It did not count that she had not been happy with her role as substitute fiancée, or that she had been trying to help Paul. Her chief emotion had been, at least in the beginning, a desire to repay Lucien for his misjudgment of her. It did not help her feelings that she had only suceeded, so far, in proving him right.

On examination, it seemed she had three options in her present predicament. She could confess the scheme to Lucien and throw herself on his mercy, hoping he would allow her to go about her business without more ado. She could defy him and watch for a nearly nonexistent means of effecting her escape. Or she could hold on to her temper, come to some kind of amicable terms with him, and wait for the end of the time period he had stipulated in the hope that he would let her go peaceably.

None of the three courses was entirely satisfactory. The first she had already rejected. The second, though the one she was most drawn toward, seemed least likely to bring about a satisfactory conclusion to the business. The third would be the hardest, but it appeared to offer the best chance of securing her eventual freedom without embarrassment. That it might also offer the greatest danger was a possibility she could not ignore after Lucien's kiss earlier.

It could not be helped. She would have to face that when she came to it. There was always the chance that taking her in his arms had been no more than the test Lucien had called it, an impulse born of their closeness at the moment. Or so she told herself.

The morning sun climbed higher. The high-ceilinged room was cooler than most modern bedrooms would have been, still even it grew stuffy after a time. Feeling grubby in the jeans and shirt she had slept in aboard the boat, Sherry showered and changed, donning a pair of shorts and a top in a cool shade of pale blue. She unpacked her suitcases, hanging her clothes away in the armoire and arranging the contents of her cosmetic case in the bathroom.

With that out of the way, there was little else to do. She could not settle her mind to reading and, as much as she wanted to avoid Lucien, she felt a growing need to be out in the open, breathing fresh air.

Leaving her bedroom door set wide for circulation, she stepped outside, moving along the front gallery. Her footsteps seemed to echo through the open house in an empty silence. She had the distinct feeling that she was alone, not a pleasant sensation in this isolated spot. Could everyone have deserted her? It hardly seemed possible, but under the present circumstances she could not be certain.

She glanced into a large, square room opening also off the gallery beyond her own. It was the living room, fitted with comfortable appointments in green and white with touches of yellow. On its far side, on the opposite corner of the house from her own, was another bedroom with a connecting study. She did not intrude beyond the door. From the austere furniture and the brown and gold color combination, it seemed certain the rooms belonged to Lucien.

The house, she discovered, was not as large as it appeared from the outside. It had only six rooms, though they were spacious ones. There was no central hall. The front entrance led into the living room, which must once have been termed a parlor. Directly behind it was the dining room. With the exception of Lucien's study, the other rooms were fitted out as bedrooms, a practical arrangement in a weekend home when guests might be expected for extended visits. The only problem was the location of the kitchen. There was none, so far as Sherry could see, though various savory aromas seemed to come from somewhere behind the house. A stairway descended from the rear of the side gallery, giving access to a small outbuilding. Sherry hesitated no more than a moment. On quick, sandalled feet, she slipped down the stairs, making her way along a brick path covered overhead by a wooden latticework breezeway. At the far end could be seen the open door of the small brick building with its overlarge chimney standing as a remnant of other times. It was an outdoor kitchen. Once, the breezeway had protected servants bringing food to the dining room from the rain. Doubtless it now protected Marie, though it occurred to Sherry to wonder why, when the house was modernized with bathrooms and electricity, an indoor kitchen had not been added to save Marie all those steps.

Inside the building, Marie could be seen moving about. Her work area appeared up to date with gleaming appliances, color-coordinated counter space, and bright lighting. The woman glanced toward the door. At the sight of Sherry, her kindly face creased in a smile. With the spoon in her hand, she gestured toward an arched opening in the breezeway which gave access to the grounds in the back of the house. Thinking that the housekeeper was inviting her to explore, Sherry nodded and, with a smile, turned in the direction she indicated.

Dipper gourds, their green globes already the shape of Mexican *maracás*, were growing on the outside of the lattice. Spreading behind the house on its high pillars was a garden of tropical appearance and fecundity, a jungle of rioting growth. Enormous elephant ears, large enough for umbrellas, grew abundantly, fronted by a long stretch of tropical ginger lilies whose exotic fragrance perfumed the air. Pausing to sniff one of the clusters of flowers, she touched a fragile white blossom like a perfect albino swallowtail butterfly.

The sun beat down on her head with a searing heat and she moved into the shade of a banana forest, craning her neck backward to see the great, leathery red blooms at the top of the tall trunks, half hidden among the waving, wind fretted leaves. Farther along there was a smaller variety of bananas with bright magenta blossoms and tiny green bananas like fingers. The lush smell of verdant growth and damp earth, mingling with the fragrance of flowers, surrounded her like incense and she stood breathing deeply, bemused with the assault on her senses of sight and sound and smell.

"All you need is a sarong," Lucien said, ducking beneath a large banana leaf and strolling toward her.

The instant she saw him Sherry realized this was what Marie had been trying to tell her, that Lucien could be found here. He had removed his shirt, letting it swing from the strong brown fingers of one hand. The slashing shadow patterns falling through the banana leaves danced across his bronzed shoulders. She wished that she had the gift of repartee, that she could think of the perfect cutting remark to wipe the amusement from his face.

"Why — why a sarong?" she asked as he stopped at her elbow.

"Because, despite the ice maiden uniform you have donned, your coloring seems to lend itself to this atmosphere. You have the look, *Chérie*, of warm passion, the smoothness of your lips, the *soie sauvage* color of your hair, wild silk to you, *petite*. Then there is the faint tilt of your enormous eyes. It all combines to give you away. You belong to the hot country, by nature if not by birth, where love and loving comes easy."

"The hot country?" she said, turning away to hide the flush that stained her cheeks from the intensity of his gaze, feigning a detachment she did not feel.

"Here, subtropical Louisiana," he said. "There are few places hotter, or with more humidity. The humidity here causes a wet heat that presses into your skin until it boils in the blood and warms the heart."

She began to walk, out of the shade of the trees and across a stretch of thick green lawn. He fell into step beside her.

Glancing at him, at the mud that spotted his pants legs and caked his shoes, she said the first thing that came into her mind to change the highly charged subject. "You look as if you have been working."

"You sound surprised."

"I suppose I am. Somehow I don't connect you with physical labor. You seem the type to sit behind a huge desk and give orders until you keel over on top of it."

"Rather than a man of action?" he queried. "It might be convenient to know that my appearance is so deceiving. You can never tell when such a thing will come in handy."

Sherry was not taken in by his innocent air. She shot him a look of loathing. When she did not comment he went on.

"No, this morning there was the small matter of a drainage ditch around his garden patch that Jules needed help digging. At this time of year we have tropical showers every evening and drainage can be important. Jules and Marie depend on their garden not only for their summer meals but also for their winter supply of vegetables."

"And you took shovel in hand," she said, her tone so scathing that a look of irritation appeared for the first time in his eyes.

"Is that really so hard to believe?"

She did not reply, for without his shirt, and with the hot sun pouring over his black hair, the harsh planes of his face and the satin glide of his muscles, he looked like a man who could, and would, do anything.

They had rounded the end of the house and were moving along a side path where great azaleas higher than their heads skirted the house, and glassy-leaved camellias pruned like trees cast a deep shade. On the opposite side stretched a hibiscus hedge, the flamboyant blossoms shading from white into pink, rose, and red into brilliant orange down its long length.

Sherry let her gaze move over the flowers, the trees, and emerald-green grass. Though she was acutely conscious of the man beside her, and of her false position where his brother and himself were concerned, she did not intend him to see her discomfiture. She would not give him that satisfaction, or that advantage.

Keeping her tones quiet, almost reflective,

she said, "Can you tell me – Lucien – why it was necessary to inform Marie and Jules that you and I – that we–"

"That we are lovers?" he supplied in some amusement as she groped for an unembarrassing phrase.

"That we are romantically involved," she finished, slanting him a harassed look tinged with chill.

"I didn't tell them. They, or at least Marie, assumed it."

"It comes to the same thing since I saw no sign that you tried to correct the wrong impression."

"No," he admitted.

"Why? Because it suits your plans?"

"I think," he said, "that you had better explain that."

"You meant for it to look as if we went away together deliberately in order to discredit me with Paul. To make him think I was easily persuaded – to desert him."

"To substitute one brother, one richer brother, for the other?"

Sherry flicked him a tight-lipped glance. "Yes."

"My reasons were not so melodramatic," he answered with a disarming smile. "To begin with, Marie was so happy to see me with a girl it seemed a shame to shatter her fond illusions. She thinks I should relax more in feminine company, though she has nearly given up the idea of dancing at my wedding. The main reason, however, was the lack of a believable explanation if I denied the obvious one. Marie and Jules know all of my relatives, and I doubt, somehow, they would accept you as a business client, especially after the scene enacted for them this morning."

"So I am to go along with everything without a thought for what my friends and working associates may think if it comes out?" she exclaimed, her temper rising in spite of her best intentions.

He swung his head to stare down at her. "That matters to you?"

She had, for an instant, forgotten his unflattering ideas of her character. They returned now with added force. "Of course it matters!"

"Loyalty is an admirable trait—"

"It isn't loyalty to Paul, at least not entirely."

"Don't tell me you are concerned for your reputation?"

"And why not? It's all very well to say that what other people think doesn't matter, but the way they treat you depends on what they think of you."

He sent her a frowning glance. When he spoke his voice was touched with mockery. "Are you by any chance implying that you have been treated unfairly?"

"Don't tell me the idea never crossed your mind?"

"Not seriously. In any case, I don't believe, at this late date, that it matters. What is done, is done."

"You don't mean you would keep me here regardless? You can't do that. It's barbaric!"

"Why? If I had waited until you had seen Paul, then invited you both to join me here, it would have been no more than a few days of relaxation, a comfortable visit. The fact that you are here alone changes nothing. Try to think of yourself as my honored guest."

"I might be able to do that if I had been given the chance to refuse your kind hospitality," she returned heatedly. "You won't get away with this. Paul will begin to wonder eventually, why I never showed up. If he gets no answer at my apartment after several tries, he's sure to check with his secretary. She will explain what happened about the plane tickets and hotel reservations. A call to the airline terminal or my hotel, either one, will give him the information that I arrived. It might also net him the connection

118

with you, his elder brother."

Lucien shrugged. "If Paul calls the hotel, he will talk to Jonathan Travers, who can be depended on to stall him. But I believe I can take care of any inconvenient inquiries Paul may make by arranging to have a telegram sent to him from the St. Louis office in your name. 'Regrets due to an illness in the family' should serve. Under such circumstances, he won't be surprised if you aren't at home to answer the phone."

"I don't have a family," Sherry said, her satisfaction at being able to disoblige him even in so small a matter plain.

"No? Thanks for the information. We will make it a close friend then."

"You think of everything."

"I try," he answered, his dark gaze direct, considering.

His assurance infuriated her. "You won't get away with this," she said gratingly, the intensity of her feelings vibrating in her voice. "You may think you will, but you won't — not if I have to see to it personally. Revenge is an ugly word, but you've introduced me to its meaning. I think if I ever get the chance that I will enjoy making you pay for what you are doing."

"It doesn't surprise me. Civilization is not

much more than skin deep in any of us. For myself, I find I'm not too far removed from my buccaneer ancestor. I don't mind your dislike at all. In fact, I consider it a challenge. I could easily come to enjoy taking what I want."

He was so close, there on the shaded path. A single step and his arms encircled her. His fingers twined in her hair, drawing her head back. His lips brushed hers lightly, almost experimentally. As she tried to jerk away, his grip tightened. The pressure of his mouth increased, becoming a firm demand. The suffocating feeling of helpless rage filled Sherry's chest, and then she was aware of nothing except the sun-warmed skin of his muscled shoulders, the tension in his hold, and the burning imprint of his lips on hers.

Abruptly, he released her. His face was expressionless, though his eyes held hers, a watchful look in their dark depths.

Sherry drew a deep breath. "You're making a mistake," she said, her tone husky.

"Am I? I doubt it. But if I am wrong I will accept the consequences — gladly."

Without giving her the time or opportunity to comment, he swung away from her and strode back along the path in the direction they had come.

What had he meant by that last cryptic statement? That question plagued Sherry long after she had returned to her room. As she lay staring into the sunburst design of the fabric lining the tester over her bed, she could not force her mind away from the incident. Had Lucien Villeré meant he would be glad to make reparation for his behavior? Or had he intended to say that he would not be sorry to see himself proven wrong in his assessment of her? Once, the only reparation for the compromising position in which she had been placed would have been marriage. Ridiculous thought. She should thank her lucky stars that this wasn't the old days when such measures would have been necessary. She could think of a great many things more comfortable than being married to a man like Lucien solely because of the dictates of propriety. She was by no means certain that he was the man to have his hand forced in such a way, even in another day and age. As he had admitted himself, in him the veneer of the gentleman was only a thin shell over the primitive instincts of a pirate.

The day before had been an exhausting one followed by a night with no more than a few hours of broken sleep. Still, Sherry did not realize she had drifted off until she came suddenly awake. Someone was in the room, moving about. It was the housekeeper. Stealthily, so as not to awaken her, the woman was closing the French windows and pulling the drapes over them to shut out the increasing heat. A delicious coolness was filling the room, like the effect of a cooling system.

Marie glanced toward the bed. Seeing Sherry's eyes open, she smiled in greeting, then said something in which Sherry caught the name of M'sieur Lucien. Giving a laugh and a resigned shrug, the housekeeper pointed toward a vent almost hidden by the fall of the drapes. Sherry nodded as she understood that M'sieur Lucien had demanded that the cooling be turned on though Marie considered it a great and deplorable waste. Electricity, Sherry thought, would be expensive way out here; it might even have to be generated on the spot.

Marie stepped to the washstand, where she pointed to Sherry's wristwatch lying on its polished surface, making pantomime gestures of eating to indicate that it was time for lunch.

"No, thank you, I don't want anything." Sherry told her, then seeing the blankness on the woman's face, gave her a firm negative, shaking her head. She had no wish to face

Lucien over the long table in the dining room.

When Marie had gone Sherry stared up once more at the sunburst design of the blue silk in the tester above her. Nothing had changed. She was still a prisoner, still no closer to persuading Lucien to let her go free. With the heaviness of sleep clinging to her still in addition to a dull depression caused by the futility of her appeals to her captor, it occurred to her to wonder if it was possible that she would never be free. Young women had been kidnapped before and disappeared, never to be seen or heard of again. The danger could not be ignored. Still, if that was the case, surely things would have proceeded differently. She would not be lying here in luxury. She would have been left behind somewhere in that twisting passage of the bayous. No, Lucien Villeré's purpose was precisely as he had stated, to get her out of the way for a few days so Paul could become acquainted again with the girl he had once loved. A laudable motive, perhaps, if Sherry had been the kind of scheming gold-digger Lucien obviously thought her to be. That Lucien himself should feel some elemental attraction to her was unfortunate. She wondered if he was as disconcerted by it as she was. It must have been the last thing he had expected.

No, she could not feature him being non-plussed over anything. Hadn't he said he was beginning to like taking what he wanted? She had not, so far, been successful at resisting him. That must change. Next time she must be prepared, or so she told herself. But, remembering the feel of his lips on hers, the hard band of his arms around her, she shivered, aware of an ache in the back of her throat.

She tried to think of Paul and of how he would react when he discovered what Lucien had done. It was no good. Paul had become a shadowy figure, his face blotted out by the sardonic smile and hard features of his brother. With a small cry Sherry shook her head, but she could not banish the image before her mind.

A knock came at the door. It was not a timid sound. There could be little doubt who was on the other side of the panel. She did not answer.

"Sherry?" Lucien called.

She turned her face away, lying very still. Here in her room she was safe from the skirmishing in which she had, until now, fought a losing battle. He would not force his way inside, she thought. She discovered her mistake as the door opened to admit his tall form. Surprise held her immobile as she watched him advance across the room to stand at the foot of her bed, his hands braced on the crosspiece.

"Sulking, *Chérie?*"

"Am I to be allowed no privacy?" she parried, pushing herself to a sitting position and glaring at him as she tossed her hair back from her face.

"Very little, else how am I to know when you might take it into your head to run away?" he replied with unimpaired good humor.

"I thought you had covered every angle, including that one," she taunted him.

"Oh, I am satisfied that you will not be able to escape me to the point of getting back to New Orleans, but I feel a certain responsibility for your safety as well. I have the feeling that you might be foolish enough to court drowning, or a slow death alone from starvation or exposure in the wetlands — if you don't meet with quicksand or snakebite. It's not hospitable, to strangers, our bayou country. My conscience could not be easy if I allowed such a thing."

"You have no conscience," she flashed at him, "and I would certainly rather trust the hospitality of the bayou to yours."

The corners of his eyes tightened but his smile did not slip. He made a gesture that encompassed his presence in her room and her own position in the bed. "I'm afraid I cannot allow you to test their relative merits. Privacy has always been an overrated commodity to those of us with Latin blood, and I would like to point out to you, if you haven't noticed, that there are no locks on the doors here at Bayou's End. I would advise you not to try a hunger strike or resort to a fit of the sullens. I will not have Marie upset, nor will I allow you to cause her the extra work of bringing trays to you when you are obviously able to come to the table." His voice dropped to a softer note. "You may look on this as a warning. I will come and get you if you try it. Now. Lunch is on the table."

"I understood that from Marie," she said after a moment, determined not to appear upset by his threats.

"Then I will expect you in the dining room in ten minutes—"

"I'm not hungry."

"—Or, if you prefer," he went on as if she had not spoken, "I will wait here for you until you make yourself ready."

"I am perfectly capable of knowing when I wish to eat."

"Are you, *Chérie*? Or are you letting mere pique get in the way of your judgment? I will expect you in ten minutes. Do not disappoint me."

"Overbearing, conceited, pompous, domineering—" she muttered to herself when the door had closed behind him. She recognized, however, that she could not win in a war of wills of this sort. She was too vulnerable here in this unlocked room to do anything other than as he had said. Also, he had some right on his side. She did not want to be a burden to Marie. It wasn't her fault that she had been saddled with an unwilling guest.

Sherry swung her feet to the floor and stepped into her sandals. Feeling tousled and untidy from sleep, she smoothed her knit top down over her hips, then moved to the dressing table where she took up a brush to bring some kind of order to her hair. A touch of lip gel, and she looked less pale, more ready to go out and do battle. The action reminded her of her earlier resolve. She was not sure what good looking her best would do, but it seemed a step in the right direction. She must try not to antagonize Lucien, which would not help her, but would serve only to keep him on guard. It would not be easy. He had done nothing but thwart her and taunt her since the moment of their meeting. She was not sure that she would be able to hide the sheer rage he aroused in her.

Lucien waited for her in the living room. Sherry forced herself to smile at him as he got to his feet at her entrance. His eyes narrowed a fraction before he glanced at his watch, congratulating her on her promptness. Together they moved toward the double doors of the dining room.

Their places had been set at the table with the main course in place and the dessert sitting ready on a serving cart to one side. There was no sign of Marie, Sherry saw, as Lucien held her chair for her to be seated. That was a great pity since it would mean she would have his whole attention.

"What became of the ice maiden?" he asked as he sat down and took up his fork.

Sherry knew it would not be wise to drop her antagonism too quickly. When she spoke it was in a controlled voice without venom. "She is still here, not quite melted by the heat, though the air conditioning, when you had it turned on, was certainly welcome."

"One of my mother's innovations. She likes her comforts," he replied.

From that inauspicious beginning they managed to keep up a species of conversation as the meal progressed. Lunch was a chef's salad with crisp iceberg lettuce, fresh tomatoes and cucumber, shrimp, and slivers of chicken breast. With it went buttered rounds of French bread, followed by chilled halves of honeydew melon heaped with fresh strawberries and sliced peaches.

At last Sherry sat back, replete. "It was all very good," she commented, "light and refreshing, lovely for such a warm day."

"Marie is a good cook. You should taste her gumbo."

"I assume that I will," she said in a cool voice just touched with wryness. She dropped her napkin in her plate, then rose from her chair, forcing him to get to his feet also.

"No coffee?" he asked.

She shook her head, unable to contemplate the black brew Marie had, in such weather, poured for Lucien. She thought for a moment he was going to argue and braced herself for the struggle. Then he shrugged.

Drifting out on the gallery where a gentle breeze wafted along the shady space, she wandered to the front of the house. There she selected a chair of white rattan filled with cushions in a cool green print and sank down into it.

His cup in his hand, Lucien joined her, taking a cane lounge at an angle where he could watch the play of expression across her face. They sat in silence. Sherry stared out over the lawn, watching the glitter of the sun on the lake through the trees with her chin lifted, though she did not realize it, in an attitude which could have been taken for a challenge.

"Hauteur doesn't suit you," Lucien said at last.

"I think you mean it doesn't suit *you*," she answered, flicking him a quick glance.

"It makes little difference to me."

There was an oblique threat in that statement, she thought, but she chose to ignore it. Nor did she make any other effort at conversation. He had brought her here against her will. She had decided not to fight him, but she was under no obligation to entertain him or to make the time she must spend in his company pleasant for him. She realized with a part of her mind that it might be better if she did so, but at this moment she could not bring herself to smile and chatter of inconsequential things.

The breeze had stopped, the air had grown still, as if waiting. The moss on the trees hung straight, dulling to the color of old men's beards as the sun went behind a cloud. A honeybee hovered around them, bumping the walls and their chairs before flying drunkenly away.

"So," he said into the quiet, "you have decided to be difficult."

It had not been her intention, but she would not give him the satisfaction of admitting it. "What did you expect? Cheerful accommodation?"

He looked at her, a strange expression in his eyes. When she could no longer hold that piercing regard, she got to her feet and moved to the edge of the gallery where she rested her head on one of the colonettes that extended from the brick supporting pillars to the roofline.

Thunder rolled, a gentle booming sound in the distance. It was quiet, so quiet that she could hear the rustle of her clothing as she breathed. It was odd to hear nothing, not the murmur of distant traffic, the click and hum of office machinery, or even the muted clatter of a low-turned radio or television. She wished that Marie and Jules would join them on the gallery, anything to break this strain.

The tension that gripped her would not allow her to be still and, pushing away from

131

the colonette, she walked along the edge of the porch like a tightrope walker over an abyss. If she was forced to endure much more of Lucien's presence she would scream, she told herself. As she reached the wide flight of steps she began to descend.

"It's going to rain," he told her lazily from where he sat watching her.

"I don't care," she answered without looking back.

6

Despite her brave words, Sherry was surprised when Lucien made no move to stop her or bring her back. As thunder grumbled again, nearer now, she grew doubtful of the wisdom of her impulse. She did not stop, however, but made her way down the sloping lawn toward the lake. It was peaceful under the trees; the gentle sighing and the creaking of their branches was a friendly sound. She could almost feel her nerves relax when she knew she was no longer under surveillance. She skirted the area of the dock, since it held such unpleasant memories, and moved along the edge of the lake farther away from the house. The rising wind lifted her hair and cooled the heat of her face and she took deep breaths of it, reveling in her sense of freedom, however transitory.

She paused for a moment to watch a blue heron perched on a stump out in the lake with his eyes fixed on the water beneath him as he fished. As she stopped she heard a furtive movement behind her. She turned sharply and Jules, a short distance away, came to an abrupt halt. She stared at him, at his arrested attitude, then as a test she moved on a few paces. He followed. Once again she stopped, and his loose-jointed stride ceased, though he looked at her with soft brown eyes that were without expression.

"I suppose your precious M'sieur Lucien is afraid that I will break and run. You may tell him from me that there is no chance of that. I will stay to defeat him at his own game."

If he understood her he gave no sign, but neither did he leave his post, though he did give a worried glance up at the sky. In that moment lightning crackled, outlining the ancient tree tops in its blue-white glare.

"Go back," she told him angrily. "Go back and leave me alone."

Jules shook his head with a soft reply that she could not understand. Once more lightning crashed, followed by a deafening roll of thunder. Even Sherry had to concede it was madness to linger under the trees with their powerful attraction for lightning bolts. A gust of wind tossed their branches and swooped low to flatten her clothing against her. With reluctance, Sherry admitted defeat. Her gaze on the darkening heavens, she turned and began to make her way back toward the house. Jules looked decidedly relieved and a flicker of a smile passed over his seamed face as if he thought she must be anxious to return to the safety and company of his M'sieur.

They were nearing the house, in sight of the gallery, when he melted away into the trees with no more sound than when he had come.

Seconds later, the rain began, great fat drops that fell from the clouds to splash and splatter around her with incredible warm wetness. Ducking her head, Sherry ran the last few yards. She hurried up the steps, arriving at the top flustered and breathless, brushing at the drops caught in her hair and jeweling her arms.

A low laugh caught at her attention. She looked up to see Lucien lounging toward her. "As fastidious as a cat," he drawled. "And I thought you didn't care about the rain."

Her first impulse was to flee, to escape his innuendo and sardonic smile. If she were to defeat him at his own game, however, she could not do so from the privacy of her room.

The clash of wits and personality she had promised herself to win could only be joined if they were together. And yet, as she stared up at his darkly handsome face and audacious smile, she found she lacked the courage. The rain, a silver curtain falling from the eaves, made of the gallery a too intimate setting, especially as she was well aware now that Jules and Marie would not intrude. In addition, her irritation with him for having her followed was too close to the surface. She would only quarrel with him.

Smiling a little then, she glanced at the water spots that clung to her skin, said she thought she needed to dry herself, and made her escape to her room.

She kicked off her shoes, removed her damp clothing and draped it in the bathroom to dry, then threw herself down on the bed. The rain, splashing in wind-driven gusts on the gallery outside and drumming on the roof, made a monotonous accompaniment for her thoughts. She pressed her hands to her eyes. She must consider tactics, decide what she was to do, how she must behave. She had never set out cold-bloodedly to pit her intelligence against a man. She knew Lucien Villeré was a formidable, perhaps dangerous, opponent to begin with, but it must be done. She could not submit passively to his designs on her; she was too uncertain of what precisely they were. No, she must remain cool but friendly, treating him always not as a personal foe but as her prospective brother-in-law. She should be attractive, but not too much so; concerned, warmly human, all the things that men admired in a woman. In this way she might foster the doubt that he was wrong about her. She did not think he was quite so certain of her position in his brother's life as he had once been. She thought it would also be a good idea to conceal her active dislike and animosity. It appeared to affect him like a challenge, spurring him to outrageous behavior. There must be no more of that. Surely there was some way to prevent it. By all rights the evening should be a time of danger.

She would put her hair up tonight. That always gave a woman a regal, less approachable appearance. And to carry that idea a step further she would wear a long dress, her white eyelet with the fresh, serene charm of a summer's day. And now, while she was relaxed and calm, she must decide on a subject or two which might provide a fund of conversation, something neither personal nor controversial. Hair style, dress, jewelry, physical attraction, wit. They were weapons, she thought wryly.

The weapons women had used for centuries. She prayed they would not fail her.

The remainder of the afternoon was spent manicuring her nails, polishing them a frosty white, and experimenting with her hair. She settled at last for a feminine mass of curls, an artfully ingenuous style that also lent itself to the atmosphere of the house. After a long bath scented with attar of roses she slipped into her dress and stood surveying the effect in the full-length mirror on the back of the bathroom door. She had not remembered that the neck-line was quite so low, but her ensemble was fairly close to what she had in mind — not too formal, in good taste, sweet but distant. Peering closer she saw a new awareness in her eyes, a look almost like pain. Strange. She felt nothing but determination. She had not the slightest inclination to cry. Not the slightest.

Reaching out for her compact of eye cosmetics, she tried to erase that look, but if anything the wash of turquoise over her eyelids served to deepen the illusion. Well then, it could not be helped. Perhaps Lucien would not notice. If he did, what of it? Let him suppose it was for the way she was being treated. The result would doubtless be nil, but she would spurn no possible weapon. If that was callous and conniving, then Lucien Villeré had no one to blame but himself.

Her last act was to pass the gold chain holding the Villeré betrothal ring over her head once more. She had grown used to its familiar weight, used to the idea that if it should prove necessary she could draw the ring from her bodice to support her claim. That she had not yet resorted to such action was due as much to pride as to the knowledge that the claim was false. Plus a suspicion that the presentation of the ring would make little real difference.

Lifting her chin, Sherry let herself out of her room. She made her way to the living room where the clatter of glassware and cutlery indicated that Marie was setting the table.

"*Très belle, mademoiselle, très, très belle!*" Marie exclaimed, laying down a handful of silver and clasping her hands. An instant later, she waved toward a cabinet, obviously posing a question. Sherry smiled and thanked her for the compliment, but she had no idea what the woman was asking of her. They were trying to communicate with gestures while Marie repeated each word slowly and loudly when Lucien came, unheard, into the room.

"She wants to know, *Chérie,* if you would like a drink before dinner. If you would she will serve it to us in the salon, or living room – a polite way to remove us from her working area, I suspect."

"That would be lovely if I could have something tall and fruit flavored," Sherry said, and waited while Lucien relayed the message. Giving him a smile that obviously surprised him, she accepted his arm and allowed herself to be led back into the living room.

He seated her in a peacock chair, that thronelike rattan chair of the tropics with its pedestal base and tall, fan-shaped back. Before her was a glass-topped cocktail table with a mass of flowers beneath the glass, the pink and purple of african violets and the brilliant red of episcias. The living room was furnished like an extension of the gallery, using the same furniture of white rattan, though here it was fitted with deep overstuffed cushions. There were a few antique pieces for a touch of permanence, a spice chest, a secretary, and a glass-enclosed bibelot cabinet containing an intriguing assortment of small antiques – snuffboxes, candle snuffers, wick trimmers, and the like. The bright yellow and cool green of the fabrics that had been used gave an effect of sunlight and leaf shadows, one that was heightened by the lush potted palms in jardinieres that flanked the fern, contributing an added tropical note.

The wood floor was polished to a bright sheen and overlaid with an oriental rug in a stark white and black design. Overhead was a large crystal chandelier that had been wired for electricity. Its lusters tinkled constantly, like delicate wind chimes, in the draft from the air conditioning.

Lucien took a chair across from her. Leaning back, he propped an elbow on the arm, surveying her with an expression in his eyes that was as unnerving as it was complimentary. He had changed for the evening also, donning a dark gray vested suit. With it he wore a shirt of some silky material left open at the neck in the Continental fashion. The look of casual elegance suited him.

Sherry summoned a smile. "It seems to have stopped raining."

"Yes," he agreed.

Now was the time for one of those conversational gambits she had so carefully committed to memory. The only trouble was, she could not recall now what they had been. True enough, she had never been in a situation quite like this one, still it was maddening, the effect this man had upon her usual self-possession.

Her difficulty was solved by the arrival of

141

Marie with their drinks, a tall, frosty glass of pineapple juice over crushed ice for Sherry, and chilled wine for Lucien. The smile the housekeeper bestowed on them before she moved discreetly from the room once more left Sherry uneasy.

She took a sip of her drink. It was delicious, fresh, sweet, and tart, without a hint of alcoholic content. And yet, she stared at it with a brooding look in her eyes. "Why," she said slowly, "do I have the feeling that I am being overpampered and overprotected?"

"Perhaps because you are oversensitive," he suggested.

"Really?" she asked in disbelief. "I don't see how you can say that with Jules following me about this afternoon like a watchdog."

"You are my guest and he was concerned for your safety."

"And also, just possibly, for the carrying out of your orders?"

"No, though I cannot accept responsibility for any misconceptions he and Marie may hold, as I told you. They are bayou country people; their lives are spent close to the earth. No one has to explain to them what is between a man and a woman." She sent him a scathing look which he ignored. "As for your reluctance to stay here with me, I expect they feel it is no concern of theirs. Because they have known and trusted me all their lives, they would be hard to convince that the problem between us is serious, much less a criminal matter. They leave it to me to settle in my own way. They may have a certain curiosity, but they wouldn't dream of interfering, any more than I would interfere in their personal lives."

"How convenient for you. And I suppose you don't call following me interfering?"

"Ah, well, Jules knew that it was much more dangerous for you out there among the trees than here in the house with me."

That was a matter of opinion, Sherry told herself, raising her glass to her lips in an effort to appear calm. Her smile was brittle when she spoke at last. "I suppose I should have expected nothing else, especially when I remember my introduction to Étienne and Estelle at the restaurant last night."

Was it only last night? It seemed such a long time ago. It was strange to think of so many people with such mistaken ideas. Her employer and fellow workers at the office, thinking she was engaged to Paul. Lucien, certain she was Paul's mistress. Étienne and Estelle just as certain she was Lucien's woman. Paul under the impression that she had failed him, gotten cold feet and backed out on their arrangement, and soon to be foisted off with a tale of a sick friend. Now Marie and Jules, carried away with the idea that she meant something special to Lucien Villeré. When would it all be sorted out. Would it ever be?

Lucien made no answer to her bitter comment. He drank from his own glass, then sat swirling the liquid it contained, a frown between his eyes. At that sign of preoccupation, Sherry felt her spirits rise. Was it possible that something she had said had penetrated his assurance? With renewed determination, she changed the subject.

"This is a pleasant place, Bayou's End. Do you come here often?"

Lucien roused himself to answer with something of an effort. "I spend most weekends here. That is, I do when I can escape from the social round. Fortunately my mother prefers Paul's escort to mine. They are more congenial."

She was oddly grateful for his cooperation in leading the conversation away from their situation.

"You prefer the bayou country to town life?"

He nodded. "Life is slower here. There is time to think without constant interruption.

There is no telephone, no mail service, only peace. If you close your eyes it's almost like going back seventy-five or a hundred years to a more placid time, a time when a man might spend his days in such quiet seclusion."

"No mail service? What of Jules and Marie? I thought they lived here the year round."

"They do, but it's too time-consuming and expensive for the postal service to bring their mail this far out. They pick it up at the Post Office in the nearest town, and at the same time they restock the pantry shelves. They make the trip every two or three weeks."

"I see. And how do they get there?"

He slanted her a grim smile in recognition of her obvious quest for information. "They use an outboard motor and one of the aluminum boats. Jules has one he rigs with cushions and a sun canopy. It's quite comfortable, or so he assures me."

"Don't they get lonesome with no neighbors, nothing to do?"

"I wouldn't know. You must ask them. Tell me, why the concern with Jules and Marie?"

"Despite everything, I – like them."

"Interesting. Are you always so quick with your likes – and dislikes."

She was about to answer in the affirmative when she saw his eyes narrow with cynicism.

The question was not one she could deny, however.

"Nearly always," she answered, and looked up with decided relief as Marie came to call them to dinner.

"We are honored," Lucien said as they sat down to the table. It fairly sparkled with china on lace placemats surrounded by gleaming silver and an assortment of water and wine glasses. The centerpiece was of white ginger lilies on a bed of fine-cut fern surmounted by a spray of white orchids with purple throats. The scent of the flowers pervaded the room.

"What do you mean?"

"Marie has actually cut a spray of her precious orchids for us. She grows them herself, from a half dozen plants that I gave her once for Christmas. She has always been wild about flowers. The gardens around the house are owing to her, not to any efforts of mine. But if I had known how attached she would be to her orchids, I would have gotten her a dozen more. She cuts them only on what she considers to be special occasions."

"You mean she cut them on my account? What a waste."

"I wouldn't call it that," Lucien corrected. "If it troubles you, try looking on it as simply a form of encouragement for me. You are the

146

first woman I have ever brought here, a state of affairs Marie considers unnatural."

Sherry, afraid the woman placing their plates before them would be puzzled or hurt by his use of her name in that dry tone of voice, smiled and complimented her on the table. When Lucien translated, Marie thanked her, but she did not linger.

Course followed course. Small cups of fresh gumbo were replaced by a fresh vegetable salad and tournedos with vegetable side dishes. This was succeeded by a dessert of fresh cherries, carefully pitted, in a brandy sauce flambé, over a dish of rich ice cream. The food was superb, requiring a great deal of attention. This was fortunate, since there was little else to provide a distraction. Lucien retreated into a brooding silence. Lacking the will or the means to draw him out of it, Sherry followed suit. Though she wanted to enjoy the meal, as it progressed her throat seemed to close. It was an effort to swallow or to reach naturally for a sip of water or taste of wine. Her silverware clattered much too loudly against her plate and there appeared to be no graceful way to cut her meat or eat the unwieldy French bread. It was a relief when the entree was removed at last and the dessert was set before them with coffee and a liqueur.

When Marie had departed once more, Sherry picked up her spoon, frowning at it in sudden doubt of her ability to do justice to the sweet. "Found something on your spoon?" Lucien asked her in a taunting undertone.

"No—no," she said. "I was admiring it. It is a beautiful set of silver." Indeed that had been one of the thoughts that had run, like sand from an hourglass, through her mind.

"The china, the silver, everything, in fact, that we have used tonight came with the house. It belonged to my great-grandmother. When the house was remodeled it was all found in crates and barrels in the attic."

"It must be valuable."

"I suppose so."

"I'm surprised you or your mother didn't take it home to New Orleans."

"It — belongs in the house. In any case, my mother was not too excited about the find. She has a great deal of that sort of thing handed down through her family for years, besides the things she had chosen as a part of her own trousseau."

"But to put it to constant use — I couldn't stand it," Sherry said with a small shudder and a wry smile for her concern.

"You needn't think that they are brought

out every day; they're not. Marie is apt to hide everything breakable and serve us out of plastic during the hunting and fishing parties we have here. I told you that you were honored."

Sherry did not know how to answer that any more than she had earlier. She grasped at the first thing that occurred to her. "Your mother — does she come here often?"

"Just as isolation isn't Paul's idea of perfect happiness, neither is it my mother's. She comes once or twice a year, usually when we have guests or a house party here, and she keeps a few things here in one of the bedrooms, in case the solitary mood strikes her. There is little chance of anyone happening upon us, if that is what you were getting at. You can forget the possibility."

"It doesn't hurt to know," she answered. If he thought she was still testing possibilities, she would not disabuse him of the notion.

"I would have told you if you had asked, and saved you a great deal of trouble."

"But what would we have found to talk about?" she asked him sweetly, spooning cherries as tasteless as ashes into her mouth.

"You, perhaps," he returned.

"I thought you were certain you knew me — or my type — too well to be interested."

He was silent a long moment, his eyes resting on her face, then he said slowly, "I might pretend otherwise, for the sake of passing a dull evening."

"It's my life you would find dull. An average childhood, safe, secure, happy, with a pair of normal, loving parents. They died when I was in high school. The rest you know: secretarial training, and then, because I have always liked the idea of ships and the sea, I applied for a job with Villeré Shipping Lines. You see? Ordinary and boring."

"Haven't you forgotten something?"

"I don't think so."

"What of Paul? Doesn't he rate a mention in the story of your life?"

For a startled moment she met his dark gaze across the table, then her lashes swept down, concealing her expression. "I've told you before," she said. "I will not discuss your brother with you."

"Because there is nothing to discuss?"

She looked up once more, her blue-green eyes stormy. "Why do you keep coming back to that? Why do you insist there can be nothing serious between us when you admitted you didn't consider Paul bound to Aimee, and must know that he feels little for her at this late date?"

"I have never known Paul to be able to keep a secret in his life. I see no reason why he should start now, especially with a woman like you. He would never have been quiet about you – your looks, your opinions, your every good point. It would have been impossible to make him be quiet."

"That's scarcely proof, is it?" she asked, laying down her spoon. "You did say that Paul had mentioned me."

He nodded. "I got the impression at the time that he was intrigued, but a little discouraged because you seemed immune to his charm. My brother has always been attracted to what he can't have. His interest usually wanes when he possesses it."

Sherry drew in her breath as the color drained from her face. "That's an ugly thing to say," she told him with difficulty, "even if you didn't mean it or believe that it is true. If you did, then it is unforgivable."

She did not trust herself to stay and wait for his reply. Pushing to her feet, she hurried from the room.

7

The soft darkness of the front gallery enclosed her. Though the air was warmer than the artificially cooled confines of the house, it offered a sense of comfort. A faint night wind stirred her curls and fluttered the hem of her dress. It brought with it the smell of dampness from the rain-wet earth and the fresh fragrance of growing things.

As the heat of the moment drained from her, Sherry's footsteps slowed. She stopped beside a colonette glimmering white in the dimness. The painted wood was cool to the touch, a smooth, rounded support.

Why had she allowed herself to become so upset? Paul's actions, his feelings for her or lack of them, held no power to hurt her. She had always known that his attitude toward love was light-hearted. Hadn't she kept him at a distance for that very reason? The truth was, it had not been Paul's attitude which had given her such pain. It had been the judgment so carelessly passed upon her by Lucien. That knowledge, under the circumstances, was more disturbing than what he had actually said to her.

The creak of a board in the gallery floor betrayed the approach of her gallant host. Despite the cover of darkness, Sherry turned her face away. Still, she was vividly aware of the moment when he stepped closer.

"The mosquitoes will eat you alive out here after dark," he said, a rough timbre in his voice.

She did not answer, staring down toward the bayou where a chorus of insects and frogs disturbed the peaceful quiet of the evening.

After a moment, he went on. "You were right. I should not have said what I did to you, regardless of my thoughts on the subject."

This, she knew instinctively, was no small concession from this man. "You are entitled to your opinion," she said finally.

"And you to your privacy. That being said, can we forget our differences and start again?"

"I suppose we will have to eventually."

"A pity, too. I almost prefer our arguments

to the polite nothings that pass between us at other times. At least when you are angry you are honest."

"And you are insulting," she returned, her tone flat.

"Granted," he admitted, and hesitated so long she thought he intended to add an explanation. He did not. "Come inside. You didn't drink your coffee. We can have it in the living room now, and that should take up a little time. If we are careful we may be able to get through the rest of the evening without resorting to violence."

His manner, tinged with reason and quiet humor, was such a change as to rouse suspicion in Sherry's mind. While walking beside him back toward the front entrance she was forced to wonder if her capitulation had been too easy. The idea was not a pleasant one. He needed no encouragement to think her easily persuaded to fall in with his wishes.

To counter such a misconception, she held herself aloof, taking care not to brush against him as he held the door for her to enter the living room. At his invitation, she poured the coffee from a tray left standing on a side table. Passing Lucien his cup, she took her own to the couch, sinking down into the soft cushions. It did not help that he promptly joined her there.

"I've just noticed," she said, her voice brittle, "that there is no television." It was as good a ruse as any for breaking the silence.

"There's a portable model around somewhere for my friends who can't bear to miss the football game on Sunday afternoons. If you come across it, feel free to make use of it."

"Radio? Stereo?"

"Built in to the wall in my bedroom."

"Convenient."

"All the comforts of home," he agreed with unimpaired patience. "I might even be able to find some dance music, if the idea appeals."

At any other time, with anyone else, she would have greeted the prospect with enthusiasm, but to go into Lucien's arms, and in his bedroom at that, was more than she was prepared to do. "I don't think so, not tonight," she said stiffly.

He did not take offense. "No rush. There will be plenty of time."

"You seem to have made Bayou's End your own," she suggested.

"By default only, since it doesn't suit Paul and my mother."

"Were you responsible for the renovation, then?"

"No, not entirely. My mother takes the

credit there, redecorating being a hobby of hers. If it had been left to me, the place would be more primitive – though with all the modern creature comforts naturally."

This last was added with such wry self-knowledge that Sherry was encouraged to ask, "Including Jules and Marie?"

"I couldn't deprive them of their livelihood," he answered in mock seriousness.

From the next room came the rattle and clatter of dishes as Marie cleared the table and removed the remains of their meal. In a few minutes she would be gone, taking the dishes away to the outside kitchen. When she had finished for the day, she would go home to Jules, no doubt, leaving Sherry here alone with Lucien in this great house.

Her coffee was growing cold. Sherry drank a few swallows, then set the cup and saucer onto the glass-topped coffee table. The strong brew did nothing to control the sudden flutter of nerves inside her.

Lucien leaned forward to set his cup beside Sherry's. Unbuttoning his suit jacket and vest, he shrugged out of them, throwing them across the back of the couch.

"That's better," he said, his firm mouth curving in a smile as he stretched, turning so that he faced her with his arm along the back of the couch. "You can relax too, you know. There's no need to be so tense. We called a truce, remember? Lean back, take off your shoes."

It was an inviting prospect, especially with him lounging at ease beside her. Perhaps he had been right earlier. Perhaps she was being oversensitive, too suspicious, looking for pitfalls where there were none. There was no reason, of course, why she should be cooperative, and yet it was impossible not to recognize that in making the passing hours difficult for Lucien, she was also making them difficult for herself. So long as she did not lose sight of the fact that he was keeping her here against her will, why not fall in with his mood?

Her shoes were sandals, wisps of white leather with fairly snug straps to keep them on her feet. After a moment's hesitation she reached down, fumbling for the buckle.

"Lift your foot," he said, and as she obeyed, slipped the sandals one after the other from her nylon-clad feet and dropped them on the rug, sending her a smile of lazy approval.

His fingers about her ankles had been warm and firm. To rid herself of their vibrant touch upon her skin she tucked her feet beneath her. His intent regard was not easy to hold. She turned her attention to his capable fingers as he began to unfasten the links from his cuffs. Seeing the direction of her gaze, he extended his wrists. "My turn."

Her hands were far from steady as she tried not to touch his hard brown wrists with their stiff black hairs. She fumbled, uncertain of how the twists of gold worked. At last she slipped them from their holes and dropped them into his outstretched palm.

"Merci, Chérie," he said, his voice deep and husky.

Her eyelashes made fan shadows on her cheeks and as she looked away, refusing to meet his eyes, he grasped her hand.

"You are not like Paul's other girls."

"No?" she asked, an unconscious query in her voice.

"No. You have a quality of stillness. There is nothing blatant about you. Your figure is not the voluptuous type that he chooses. Not that it isn't lovely, but you have a tender symmetry, the kind of perfection that does not usually appeal to my brother."

Sherry was by no means sure that she enjoyed this analysis of her shape and personality. It made her too conscious of herself, of the material gently shaped to her breasts, and her skirt that clung to the curve of her hip and thigh.

"You mean, I think, that I don't strike you as being desirable."

He frowned. "Obvious allure is best left to stage personalities, bar girls, and insecure teen-agers trying to be women. You strike me as being a lady."

It was a lovely compliment and she could not help being pleased, and yet she was not certain she liked the idea. Seeing the arrested expression on her face, he chuckled. "A sensuous lady," he said, smoothing his thumb caressingly over the pulse that throbbed in her wrist, watching with enjoyment the color that slowly stained her shoulders and cheeks, rising to her hairline.

"Chérie, Chérie," he sighed, and she thought the amusement in his voice was for himself as well as for her. "A girl who can still blush. For the first time in my life I find myself envying Paul something, his possession of you."

Anger, more at his enjoyment of her confusion than for his words, touched her. "I am not Paul's possession."

"Oh? I thought you and he had pledged your undying love."

"There is a difference between being *loved*" – she emphasized the last word – "and being possessed."

A dangerous light sprang into his black eyes. He reached for her with the assurance of a man unused to resistance. "Oh yes," he said, drawing her inexorably into his arms. "But I'm not sure you truly know the difference — yet."

"No," she whispered, a terrible fear spreading through with the aching pain of poison. "No," she said again but the protest was smothered against her parted lips as his mouth came down over hers.

Her arms were pressed against his chest, stilling movement. She was caught so tightly she could hardly breathe. The soft cushions of the back of the couch cradled her head, preventing her from evading his kiss.

Abruptly, he raised his head. Her heart pounded, shaking her breast as it rose and fell. Her breath came quickly through her throbbing lips. She stared up into his eyes that were dark with passion and something else that bordered on amazement.

Lowering his head once more, he pressed his lips to the corner of her mouth, trailing fire along her cheek to the tender softness of her neck. With strangely gentle fingers he pushed the sleeve of her dress off her shoulder. As she flinched, the steel grip of his arms tightened.

"Your skin," he whispered, "has the sheen of satin." He pressed his lips into the hollow of her shoulder just above the curve of her breast.

She was enveloped in the scent of the aftershave he used and the warmth of his skin. She could feel her strength, her will to resist, leaving and a treacherous response struggling to begin. But she could not submit to it, she would not.

"But – you don't like me!" the words were a cry of protest. "You don't like the kind of woman I am."

His lips brushed delicately along the angle of her jaw, but when he answered there was a tremor of laughter in his voice. "My dear girl, how can you believe that I still cling to such prejudice?"

Though he still held her firmly there had been an easing of the intensity of the moment and so she tried again.

"Don't – don't you have any qualms about making love to the woman your brother loves?"

At last he raised his head. "If I thought – but no," he went on, his voice quiet. "He will care for sweet Aimee as much as it is in his nature to care for any woman. Being the kind of girl she is, she will never question his infidelities, or his right to them, while you, *Chérie*, would die slowly inside."

Though Sherry was not certain Lucien's estimation of his brother's character was right, his idea of her own was so close that it was disconcerting. She turned her face away. "I find your concern touching," she told him. "Especially at this moment."

His brows came together in a frown and his eyes grew hard. "At this moment? What do you know of it? You think you understand the feelings that move me, and yet how can you when I hardly understand them myself?"

Once more he took her lips. His arms slipped behind her back, lifting her to lie across his lap. Her senses whirled as he shifted position and she felt the yielding upholstery of the couch now beneath her shoulders. She stiffened as panic beat up into her mind with a strange sense of hurt.

With sudden strength, she dragged her mouth from his, arching her back, pushing against him, desperate to be free of his weight. Then his strong hands caught her wrists. Supporting himself on one elbow, he pinioned her hands on either side of her body. Head back, he stared down at her flushed and rebellious face.

Abruptly he gave a soft exclamation, the

breath leaving his lungs as though he had been struck a sharp blow. His gaze had drifted from her lips down the curve of her neck to the bodice of her dress. There, exposed to view by their struggles, lay the Villeré betrothal ring, its blue enamelwork and diamonds shining against the creamy softness of her skin.

Slowly the fingers of his right hand unclamped from her wrist. Unwillingly, or so it seemed, he forced himself to reach for the piece of jewelry, turning it this way and that in the light.

"Why?" he said at last, a note of strain in his voice.

She did not pretend to misunderstand. "Why not," she asked, "when you were so determined to think the worst of me?"

"That isn't an explanation."

It was true enough, but despite her position, some stubborn impulse, abetted by a residue of anger at his treatment of her, prevented any inclination toward confession. She lifted her lashes in a slow sweep, her deep blue eyes meeting his squarely.

"Why should I explain to you? Why should I seek your approval, or care what you think? You mean nothing to me."

He stared at her a long moment while the

color receded beneath the bronze tone of his skin. A muscle twitched in the side of his jaw. He dropped the ring, then on a sudden surge of strength came to his feet. Reaching down, he dragged her upward, holding her for an instant while she regained her balance, then dropping his hands as though her skin were hot to the touch.

"You had better go to your room, now, before I change my mind," he said, plunging his hands into his pockets.

The smile that twisted his lips hurt Sherry in some peculiar way. She felt the need to withdraw her hasty words, to erase the doubt she saw in his eyes. Before she could do anything so foolish, she swung away from him. Lifting her skirt, she hurried from the room.

Mechanically she took off her dress and hung it carefully in the armoire, took down her hair, and slipped into her nightgown. Lying in bed, she stared with hot dry eyes into the darkness, her breathing shallow against the ache in the region of her heart. It was some time before she slept.

She awakened at dawn. As her eyes grew accustomed to the dim light, she went still like an animal in the presence of danger. Someone stood beside her bed, staring down at her.

"I only came to bring you these," Lucien said, dropping her sandals on the bedside table, "and to say good-bye." He leaned to place a hand on the bed at either side of her head. His intention was plain. She turned her head and his lips brushed the softness of her cheek.

There was a tense moment. Sherry waited, every nerve tingling with strain, for his retaliation.

Then he was gone, his footsteps sounding across the polished boards and along the gallery. In a few minutes she heard the roar of the cruiser's motor.

She reached the window in time to watch the boat move slowly from the lake into the narrow channel of the bayou, its white paint gleaming in the first light of the rising sun.

8

Quiet returned to the bayou as the roar of the cabin cruiser's motors died away. The iridescent wake left by its passing rolled into shore, and the water was still once more. A faint breeze stirred the gray moss on the trees. A cardinal flitted among the oaks, a bright flash of color in the early-morning light. Nothing else moved. It was as though the life had gone out of the place, leaving it suspended in time, waiting for the presence of one man to bring it back to life.

A ridiculous fancy. Turning sharply, Sherry moved back to the tester bed. She climbed in and pulled the sheet up to her chin, closing her eyes with determination. It was no good. She could not go back to sleep. Memories of the past two days crowded in upon her, no matter how hard she tried to keep them at bay. Over and over, the details flickered through her mind.

How could she have been so stupid as to be lured to this place? How was it possible that he could keep her here? The day before she had been stunned by the situation and deterred, in no small measure, by the watchful presence of the master of Bayou's End. Something about him, his self-control, his ruthless carrying out of a plan that must have been concocted on the spur of the moment, his fearless acknowledgement of his lawlessness, had inhibited her. She knew she attracted him, and it pleased him for the moment to play a cat and mouse game with her, but she thought that if she caused him too much irritation it would not be beyond him to use physical restraint upon her. The house could be much more of a prison than it was.

Now that Lucien had gone, leaving her in the keeping of Marie and Jules, surely there was some way she could get away from them. But if she decided to try, she wanted to be very certain that the attempt would be successful. She did not care for the idea of facing his wrath if she failed.

Her thoughts strayed to the white boat cruising somewhere on the twisting bayous, heading toward New Orleans. He had gone, she supposed, back to his office and the demands of his wide-ranging business. It was Monday, time to get back to work for him. There would be things he needed to see to, perhaps, things he could not allow to go undone.

One of the first items he would take care of, she imagined, would be to see to the sending of the telegram that would forestall a search for her, the telegram to Paul. She did not like to think of it, of the look on Paul's face when he read that poor excuse. She doubted if he would be taken in by it. He was much more likely to think she had gotten cold feet and left him to work out his problem with Aimee on his own. So long as it discouraged Paul from trying to contact her, however, what did it matter? Lucien would have won — again. Lucien. She could not imagine him accepting such a rejection. He would be much more likely to catch the first plane north to demand an explanation. Failing to find her in St. Louis, he would leave no stone unturned until he located her and received her explanation. Or would he? He had made no attempt to force an explanation from her the night before. None at all.

The trend of her thoughts was far from restful. She swung out of bed and put on her clothes before wandering out onto the gallery. It was there that Marie found her, standing staring out over the lake, when she came to call her to breakfast.

Sherry did not feel hungry. All she really wanted was a cup of coffee. It was too late to try to communicate that fact to Marie, however, since the housekeeper had already prepared the meal. She rose and followed her into the dining room.

For a time she thought that Marie's silence, her unsmiling demeanor, was the reflection of her own mood. At last it was borne in on her that Marie was displeased. Did she know then what had happened between Lucien and herself? That hardly seemed possible unless the woman was a witch, and yet something was on her mind. Was she distressed that Lucien had gone away and left her? Did she see her employer as a laggard in love? The wry smile brought about by this idea faded as Sherry examined another thought. The woman might feel Sherry was the one lacking since it appeared she could not hold Lucien at her side.

More useless fancies. What difference did it make what Marie thought? With the language barrier between them, the housekeeper could never stand as an ally with Sherry against her employer even if she wanted to.

Returning to the front gallery after breakfast, Sherry discovered Jules working down around the dock, mowing and clearing the high grass from beneath the lakeside pilings. He looked up as she descended the front steps, and from then on, throughout the day, she was aware of his watchful surveillance. When she walked through the tropical gardens he found it necessary to prune the hibiscus. When she continued around the back he felt the need of a cold drink from the kitchen. She was tempted from sheer exasperation to dive headlong into the wooded swamp area surrounding the house if for no other reason than to see what he would do. She resisted the urge, however. It was not Jules' fault. He was only Lucien's instrument.

But as she strolled on, completing the circle of the house, she caught sight of something she had not noticed before. Set back from the bayou's edge, partially screened by the trees, was a small building. Since she had nothing else to do, and curiosity was strong, she walked toward it.

Tightly built, painted white with a gray roof, it was even tinier than she had first thought. Its double doors, almost like a doll's garage, sported a large, shiny new lock.

Standing on tiptoe, she peered through the building's one small window. The interior was dark but she could just make out a rack on which hung boat seats, life jackets, and ski belts. An outboard motor hulked in one corner, fastened to a sturdy stand, while cane poles were fitted into a holder along the length of one wall. Bait cages and boxes filled a wheelbarrow, and near the doors stood a collection of gardening tools.

Her face was grim as she turned to the door to inspect the shining new lock. There was no question of carelessness, however, and she rattled the bit of brass with a derisive smile before she turned away. It was an unnecessary precaution. What good was that motor to her? She doubted very much that she could lift it to carry it from the boat house to the dock, even if the boats to use it on had not been chained to a tree. Of course it was possible that she might have secreted one of the sharpened hoes about her person and attacked Marie and Jules with it, or at least threatened to decapitate them if they didn't carry her to civilization!

No, she was not that near to going berserk. Though on second thought she was not sure that it wouldn't come to that.

She returned to the house. To escape the

feeling of being under constant observation, she sought the cool seclusion of the living room. Her gaze passed over the couch. Marie had already cleaned this morning. No dented cushions, no empty coffee cups were left as reminders of the evening before. Regardless, the events that had taken place were vivid in Sherry's mind. With a shake of her head to banish the unwelcome memories, she moved away.

She wandered moodily around the room, touching the slub texture of the green antique silk drapes, running her fingers along the hard, glasslike polish of the secretary. In one drawer of it she found stationery, heavy parchment embossed with a trio of initials so intricately intertwined it was nearly impossible to tell what they were, though she suspected the monogram belonged to Lucien and Paul's mother. Nothing else of interest met her questing gaze, only rubber bands, paper clips, and pens that would no longer write. Foiled again, she mused. She could not even send a note in a bottle bobbing along the bayou.

She knew she was prying, but she didn't care. Lucien did not deserve to have his privacy left inviolate. Besides, she told herself, self-preservation, not curiosity, dictated her actions. Anything she could learn about him might be of use as protection.

The bibelot cabinet was an intriguing piece of furniture and she stood for some time, with her fingers touching the glass, looking at the many beautiful objects it contained. There were three deep drawers in the bottom of the cabinet. Sliding the top one open, she discovered a number of extra antiques that could be brought out to vary the items on display. To assert herself and to mark her presence, she chose a piece of scrimshaw on a block of ebony, a walrus tusk carefully etched with a clipper ship under a cloud of bellied sails. She set it in place on one of the lighted shelves, removing an uninspired coral Buddha and banishing it to the drawer. The substitution might have been childish, still it was oddly satisfying.

On the wall near the cabinet hung a trio of miniatures, a man, a woman, and a sailing ship done in time-faded pastels. The man, though dressed in the style of more than a hundred and fifty years ago, had the unmistakable look of a Villeré. Was this the ancestor who had founded the family fortunes with his skill on the high seas? If so, the woman must be the girl he had captured and made his wife. In the way of most old portraits, it was difficult to tell much about her, though her hair appeared to have been golden brown, and it seemed there was strength and a touch of humor in the gentle curves of her mouth.

What had she thought, what had she felt when she was carried away by her corsair? At least there could have been little doubt of his purpose. Frowning, Sherry turned away.

Here was the door to Lucien's bedroom. She paused, catching her lip between her teeth before she opened the panel and stepped inside.

The bed had been freshly made, its covers stretched taut without a wrinkle — much less the impression of his body upon it.

On the wall beside the bed was a book cabinet with the television and the stereo he had mentioned. An assortment of records stood on the edge beside the stereo, classical, mood music, a few male and female vocalists. The books were evenly divided between leisure reading, the adventures and mysteries suitable to a weekend retreat, and business publications having to do with his varied interest. She chose a couple of the mysteries and, tucking them into the crook of her arm, turned toward the door. With one hand on the knob, she swung back. There was nothing in the neat emptiness of the room to indicate what kind of man Lucien was. It revealed little of his personality, and less of the mental processes which might have led him to kidnap a woman, take her away into the bayou country, and leave her there.

She sat reading through the day, stopping only for lunch. The book was a refuge, a tranquilizer for her strained nerves, a palliative for her troubled thoughts. It was such a successful one she hardly noticed the afternoon shower that blew up in a matter of minutes, and was just as quickly gone. The hours passed with a slow pace at first, but then as the sun started to sink down the sky they took wing. Her fears began to revive. Taking her novel, she moved out onto the gallery. Now and then she would glance up, listening, staring down the narrow waterway before the house. Would Lucien return, or would she be left alone in the house as night fell? She had never been afraid of the dark before, but this was different, this isolated old house surrounded by the inhospitable wetlands. She was not certain which she dreaded more, Lucien's return, or his failure to come.

The sun burned a red-hot path across the water of the lake in a last flare of heat before it sank down behind the dark silhouetted forms of the trees. From below the horizon it sent flares of orange and pink spreading across the sky. The dying light streaked a low-lying cloud bank of blue-gray with a tracery of gold before turning the water before her to liquid opaline.

By that time, Sherry had finished her second book and thrown it aside to watch the last hurrah of the setting sun.

The sound of the boat was a distant hum at first. It grew louder, impinging upon her consciousness, destroying the aura of contentment that the beauty and silence had drawn around her.

Her nerves tightened like coiled springs, her fingers clenched on the arms of her chair, and she stared at the point beyond the trees where the boat would first come into view. Then it was there, its sound tearing across the tranquility, its movements shattering the surface of the water, breaking it into a thousand ripples.

The moment she was sure it was Lucien's boat she slipped from her chair and moved quietly, covered by the gathering dusk under the overhanging roof, into the salon. Inside, she moved to the window and pushed aside the drapes to watch as he brought the boat smoothly into the dock. Jules appeared as if conjured out of the dimness to fasten the mooring lines, then Lucien leaped ashore. He stayed to speak a few words with Jules, his eyes scanning the house, before he moved with purposeful steps up the incline.

Sherry dropped the fold of the curtain and stood back, her hands clutching her arms.

And then, in that last few seconds before he reached the house, she took stock of her action. Was she that afraid of him? It was very well to tell herself that she did not wish to appear eager to greet him, but her retreat had all the marks of cowardice. What had she gained? If he wanted to find her, this was the first place he would look. It would be far worse for him to find her cowering in the darkness than to have him think her anxious to see him.

With disdain for her lack of composure, she squared her shoulders and moved toward the door, passing through it as Lucien reached the top of the steps.

He stopped as he saw her. The expression on his face was lost in the dimness, but she could see his arrogant stance, his air of a freebooter surveying his prize. She stiffened.

"So you came back," she said in her coldest voice.

"Did you think I would not? If you really expected me to go away and forget about you,

you must have a poor idea of your powers to fascinate."

"Are you fascinated?" She had thought to sound contemptuous, but even to her own ears the query had a ring of curiosity.

"As a lion-tamer entering a cage. I never know what trick you will try next."

"And you are sure you are a match for them all?" His jibe lent her voice a sharper edge.

"I have been, so far. But come," he said moving toward her. "You haven't said hello."

As he crossed the short space between them, she saw a watchful light in his eyes coupled with a look of intent appraisal, almost as though he were seeing her for the first time. Then he caught her shoulders.

At the last moment she turned her head away, avoiding his lips. Her face like stone, she stared over his shoulder.

"My dear Sherry," he said, his voice low, and yet carrying an undercurrent of steel. "Listen carefully to what I have to say. What I will tolerate in the morning, while you are flushed and rosy with sleep, is a very different thing from what I will take after a hard day. Don't turn from me with that look of long suffering or I refuse to be responsible for the consequences!" And while she stared at him with a feeling of suffocation closing her throat,

178

he tipped her chin and kissed her slowly, with a lingering enjoyment, though whether it was of the taste of her lips, or of the lesson she could not tell.

He released her as a soft step came near them on the gallery. Drawing Sherry into the curve of his arm, he turned to greet Marie as she came toward them with a tray of drinks.

He talked to the housekeeper in comfortable amiability as he accepted a tall, frosty glass. With a wave of his hand, he indicated that he wished Sherry to join him, relaxing in the chairs on the gallery. She did so with an odd sense of pain around her heart. As the liquid syllables flowed about her, she took her glass and stared out at the twilight, listening instead to the cicadas in the trees and the croak of the bullfrogs down by the lake.

Noticing her withdrawal, Lucien turned to her after a moment. "Marie says she is surprised and delighted that I returned so quickly. I'm sure those are your sentiments also."

It was a moment before she spoke and then she would not look at him. "Considering that it took us half the night to get here when we came, and that you have done it twice in one day and, I suppose, taken care of your business as well, I think I can agree that I am surprised."

"You think I took the long way before?"

"It crossed my mind."

"You wrong me. It is a slower trip by night along the bayou when you cannot see farther than your light will reach. Then, today I had no passenger, and didn't have to dawdle along so she could get her beauty sleep."

He was laughing at her again, satisfied that he had proven his point a few minutes earlier.

He thanked Marie with a nod of dismissal. As the woman turned to go, he made a quick request that even Sherry recognized from the tone as an order to hurry dinner.

When the woman had gone Sherry turned her face away, making no effort to ease the silence. She felt sullen. She realized that she was sulking, but he brought out the worst in her. Moreover, sulking was one of the few ways she had of retaliating. He could force his attentions upon her but he could not force her to respond or to show enthusiasm for his company.

He did not appear to notice her attitude. He lounged, totally relaxed, in his chair, staring out through the trees with unseeing eyes, a faraway look on his face. Not a word passed between them as the darkness slowly thickened.

"The mosquitoes are gathering for dinner,"

he told her, straightening at last. "And I for one am just as hungry as they are. I had breakfast here, I know, but I don't remember having lunch at all."

A cool shower was refreshing. After dusting with a scented bath powder and slipping into her underclothes, Sherry stood before the armoire, considering what to wear. The idea of dressing formally again was abhorrent. It crossed her mind to make herself as inconspicuous and unattractive as possible and yet, like her retreat into the salon this evening, that course seemed cowardly.

She chose at last a sundress in a soft apricot and white cotton. It was casual and feminine at the same time, modern and yet old-fashioned. Her hair she left free, brushing it back away from her face to hang in loose waves down her back. She used makeup carefully, touching an apricot gel to her cheeks as well as her lips. Hesitating over her jewelry case, she decided at last on a pair of gypsy bangle bracelets, her gold chain, and wide hoop earrings of burnished gold. If to call attention to herself was courageous, she told herself with a wry smile, then this was courage with a vengeance. Shaking her hair back with a defiant gesture, she left the room, making her way to the dining room.

A grape had fallen from the centerpiece of heaped fruit on the table and she leaned over the chairs to remove it from the white perfection of the cloth. She heard a step behind her and then a strong arm came around her waist and she found herself pinned against Lucien's hard, muscular frame.

"You look like a peach, cool, delicious, and good enough to eat," he murmured. And, carefully brushing her hair aside, he kissed the nape of her neck, then nipped the tender skin between his teeth. A cry of surprise broke from her lips and she twisted around. He released her, but only so he could drop a swift kiss on her parted lips as she swung to face him.

His eyes were alive with laughter. He too seemed refreshed. He wore a yellow sports shirt open at the neck with trim brown slacks, and his hair was sleeked to his head, still wet from his shower. She realized how very handsome he was, especially in this mood, and she found her own mouth curving into a smile as she met his bright gaze.

An instant later she drew away from him, aware suddenly of how near she was to forgetting her antagonism. Could her defenses be breached by a playful joke and a grin? She did not like to think so.

9

The dinner Marie served to them was good, but it lacked the flair of that prepared the evening before. In a way Sherry was grateful for the plainer fare, the jambalaya rich with sausage, oysters, shrimp, tomatoes, and herbs; the home-baked loaves of French bread, the garden fresh vegetables, and the plain dessert of fruit and cheese. It made the occasion less important, and therefore easier.

Lucien was in a mellow mood. Sitting at the head of the table with her on his right, he played the relaxed host, encouraging her to talk about her job. He listened keenly as she spoke of the operations of the St. Louis office. His interest extended to her afterwork hours also, and she found herself telling him of some of the excursions she and Paul had made, of picnics in the country and waterskiing on the Mississippi, of dinners and plays they had enjoyed. It appeared he was making an effort to get to know her, to understand her relationship with his brother. At the same time, there was a personal element in his interrogation which Sherry found disturbing.

Replete with good food, they pushed back their plates. He leaned to offer her the cheese board, and she shook her head.

"I couldn't. If I stay here much longer with nothing to do but eat, I'll be as round as a barrel."

"Perish the thought," he said, "though it looks to me as if you have a long way to go." Smiling, he reached out to lift her arm by hooking a finger through her wide bangle bracelet. "You see, too large."

Suddenly he went still as he saw the bruises that marred the soft flesh under her wrist. With a gentle finger he traced their extent. Though he caused her no pain, she flinched, afraid that he might.

"*Chérie,*" he said, his voice serious, without humor or sarcasm. "Believe me when I say I am sorry for these. I did not mean to hurt you. If I had known — but I did not. Though I have never brought a woman here before, there have been a few who have made it plain they would not object to spending time here in luxury with me. I thought once you were here, once you saw there would be no chance for you with my brother, you would settle down and enjoy your stay. I misjudged you; this I freely admit. It does not change the basic problem, however. You are here, and I still believe it is for the best. That being the case, would it be so difficult for you to consider yourself my guest for the next few days?"

"Yes!" She had to interrupt that beguiling voice. "It is impossible. I refuse to be coaxed into doing what you want. What's the difference in being your guest or your prisoner, if I'm not free to leave? Because you made a mistake, am I supposed to forgive you and become a willing hostage?"

An arrested look appeared in his eyes, as though he found her answer disturbing. She thought he was going to make another appeal, but the impulse faded. Still, she could have sworn he hesitated, uncertain how to proceed, before a hard mask of determination closed over his face.

"The trouble with you, *Chérie,*" he said, as he stripped the grapes from their stems and crushed them between his teeth, "is that you are spoiled."

"I'm spoiled?" she exclaimed. "It was you who took the law into your own hands and brought me here. It is you who are keeping me here in the most arrogant determination to have your own way that I have ever seen!"

"Oh – well, perhaps I'm spoiled too," he conceded handsomely. "We were speaking of you, however."

Mollified against her will, Sherry was forced to ask, "And how am I spoiled?"

"You are attractive, but you are so used to the idea, to the sensation of being beautiful, that you forget it. Still, you can't escape the consequences. You are used to the attention you have received all your life from men and boys, so used to it that you take it for granted. It probably never crosses your mind that they are paying homage, and yet unconsciously you expect it."

"That isn't so!"

He threw the grape stem onto his plate and dried his fingers on his napkin.

"It's true, *Chérie*, of all beautiful women. You needn't think I am attacking you personally. I am only pointing it out in the hope that you will change. But isn't it so? You have never once, since I brought you here, expressed surprise that I would want to take you in my arms. Have you never been grateful that a man wanted you?"

"I've never met a man I've been that

desperate about." The statement was bald but she hoped its plainness would put a stop to this conversation. For a moment she thought it had.

He got to his feet and pushed his chair back under the table, then stood with his hands on the back. "Not even Paul?" he queried softly.

Once more she had allowed anger and irritation to make her forget the role she was playing. It was no wonder he was suspicious. For the moment, however, there seemed no possible answer except the one she had given before. Rising abruptly, she turned away from the table and the mocking gaze of the man who watched her. "My love life is none of your business," she told him.

"But what of Paul?" he insisted as they moved along the gallery together. "You haven't asked me about him; if I saw him today, or how he was doing."

"Would you tell me if I did?"

"Certainly. When I left him, he was fine. He got your telegram this afternoon, just before I was ready to leave the office."

"And?" Her voice sounded strange, unconcerned, as if the telegram had no connection with her.

He did not answer immediately. Some

quality in his silence made Sherry glance at him. In the glow of moonlight beyond the overhanging roof she could just see the faint smile that curved his mouth. "He was – quiet, at first. He didn't want to talk about it. I suppose he was embarrassed after his announcement of your engagement last week over the phone. Eventually, he told me."

"What – what did he say?" Considering Lucien's calm demeanor and his offer to send her home, it seemed unlikely that Paul had confessed their subterfuge; still it was better to be sure.

"That you weren't coming to New Orleans because of a friend in the hospital, that he had given you the betrothal ring in a mood of defiance. What else is there to tell?"

"He could have said he loved me and was certain I would come as soon as I could."

"He could have, but he didn't. By the time I finished explaining the telegram to him as coming, probably, from a girl who felt she was getting in too deep, he seemed resigned."

Sherry swung to look at him, her honey-blonde hair spilling over her shoulder. "Getting into what too deep?"

"Matrimonial waters, of course," he answered, lifting a brow. "Be honest, *Chérie.* Don't you find the prospect of being a member of the Villeré family a bit overwhelming?"

"Not at all," Sherry answered with a lift of her chin. "So long as the — the man I love is at my side."

A frown appeared between his eyes. He was the first to look away.

The gallery echoed to their footsteps. After a moment Sherry said, "I can't believe you actually sent that telegram."

"Oh yes, I sent it. We are quite safe now from interruption — for a little while."

"We? You needn't include me in your conspiracy!"

"I'm afraid you are included, *Chérie,* whether you want to be or not. We are in this together for the next few days."

She ignored his comment. "Do you mean you plan to stay here tomorrow, not go into New Orleans?"

"Precisely. Aren't you honored?"

She sent him a speaking look. "What did you tell them at home to account for your absence?"

"Why should I tell them anything?"

"I had the idea, I suppose from Paul, that you were the nose-to-the-grindstone type. Your family must find it surprising that you are taking off from work before the week has started."

"They will have a certain curiosity, I imagine, but I doubt they will ask. Paul had too much reticence to pry into my affairs – a characteristic I have been at great pains to nurture in him since he was a child nearly ten years my junior. As for my mother, she will not risk the embarrassment. They were neither of them born yesterday. I'm sure they will be able to figure out for themselves that I'm not going away just because I want to be alone."

"What you're saying is that you do as you please without caring what they think."

"You could put it that way. However, if you think they will lie awake tonight worrying you are mistaken."

They were nearing the steps, and with a touch on her arm he guided her down them and out into the warm, soft darkness. She took a deep breath and let it out slowly, trying to ease the tension that drummed along her nerves, to ease also the sense of compulsion that permeated their relationship. She was compelled to stay here, but nothing else. Surely nothing else.

The semitropical night closed around them like the folds of a cloak. They moved from one dark tree shadow to the next, walking in pools of blackness. The night orchestration of the insects and frogs was around them also, a muted accompaniment to their steps, falling gradually into the background until it was barely heard. It left a sense of silence, and yet there was an intimation of primitive life. The stars hung low above the tops of the distant trees, peering now and then between the leaves of the green canopy above them. A breeze had sprung from nowhere, whispering among the trees, stirring the soft curls around her face. That it had discouraged the mosquitoes was evident. For the moment they were left unmolested.

They stopped near the water's edge, the lap of the gentle waves at their feet. The moonlight glistened on the water, turning it to polished silver.

She breathed deeply again but this time it was a sigh for the beauty of the night. Lucien, as if sensing her mood, said, "We miss half the wonder, half the pleasure of living, by sleeping the night away."

Though he had spoken her own sentiments, Sherry did not wish to admit it. She shrugged. "What else is there for us to do? We are made that way. We need to rest in the dark hours."

"We seldom sleep from necessity, most of us, only from habit. Our habits are learned in childhood. We could retrain ourselves to get the most from the short time we have."

"That's all very well, if we have something interesting or important to do. How would you suggest I occupy myself here to get the most from my precious time?" She spread her hands in a futile gesture indicating the emptiness of the day that she had spent and those that stretched before her. "Sleeping is as good a way as any of passing the time."

"I can see that I will have to plan some amusement for you. Tomorrow, for instance, we can go fishing." He glanced at her from the corner of his eye. "What?" he mocked. "No chorus of joy? Doesn't the prospect thrill you?"

"That will be fun," she said. "I haven't been fishing in ages, not since I was a little girl."

"Anything to get out of the house? What a wife you will make!"

It was not a compliment.

"I don't know why you should think that I would despise fishing," she told him stiffly. "I enjoyed it when I was a child. I would like to get out of the house, but so would you too if you were being forced to stay. That's human nature, I would think."

"And you are very human, aren't you, *Chérie*?"

"I'm not sure what that is supposed to mean."

"Neither am I," he admitted after a long moment. "It had something to do with honesty – and that is strange, is it not?" He stared at her in the dimness. She could hear still the echo of mockery in his voice but she could not tell whether he mocked her or himself.

"One thing more, *Chérie*," he went on. "I can't bear a complaining fishing companion. Take it as a warning."

"You prefer one who suffers in silence then, one who bows submissively to your every whim? I'm sorry, but you should be more careful whom you kidnap!"

"Ah, well," he said, and she could hear laughter threading his voice. "It could be that a little temper is more exciting."

He drew her into his arms, ignoring her resistance, controlling it with easy strength. He brushed his lips burningly across hers, then took them. Panic beat like the wings of a bird in her mind as she found herself drowning in a soft languor, yielding to the planes of his body until she was molded against him, her lips softening, parting beneath his. She clung to him, confused by the fearful longing that grew inside her.

He drew back, the laughter gone out of his face. "Yes," he said, "temper has its points.

And yet, I advise you never to cease fighting me."

In silence they retraced their footsteps. They paused on the gallery outside her bedroom door.

"We leave early," he told her. "Don't oversleep." With a last light kiss from her warm lips, he turned and walked away, leaving her alone. She stared after him, a frown of perplexity between her eyes at his change of attitude. Then with a soft sound of relief she turned and went inside.

The morning dawned soft and clear. Their footsteps left a trail through the dew-wet grass as they walked down to the boat. The purr of the cruiser was loud as it moved slowly from the dock, pushing aside wisps of the mist that hung just above the water. Sherry shivered a little. It was cool with the dawn and the breeze of their passing. The sun had not yet risen to bring warmth to the air and burn away the low-lying fog. She stood beside Lucien and an excitement moved within her as though she were beginning a new adventure with the man beside her.

"This isn't the way to the bayou," she said. They had made a wide circle and were moving up the lake.

"There's something I wanted to show you first."

"Oh?"

He slanted her a glance, a smile cutting into the firm planes of his cheeks. "Wait and see."

The lake made a wide, lazy curve. They moved out of sight of the house, following a channel cut between the towering cypress trees growing in the water. A few minutes more and Lucien cut the motor, letting the boat glide to a drifting stop. Ahead of her at the edge of the lake Sherry saw a crude platform of rough lumber built out over the water. From the platform came muffled squawking and the flutter of wings. And then, as they cleared the low branches obstructing their vision, she saw a cloud of white.

"Oh — cranes," she said.

Lucien shook his head. "Close. Actually they are snowy egrets, a species of heron. Until just a few years ago they were nearly extinct, down to less than two dozen birds. Then a number of the residents along the bayous near the coast began to colonize them, arranging places like this, breeding grounds to protect them and encourage them to multiply. You may have heard of Avery Island? It is owned by the McIlhenny family. It has become a famous tourist attraction with extensive gardens where hundreds of rare plants from the four corners of the world are grown. Edward A. McIlhenny originated the first egret nesting site on Avery Island. He was also the first to introduce the nutria, a fur-bearing South American rodent much like our native muskrat, only larger and more prolific, to Louisiana. He was quite a conservationist."

"Snowy egrets. It's a lovely name. It seems so appropriate somehow. But there are so many birds. Not all of them are egrets, are they?"

"No, some are white cranes. There are blue cranes too, as well as ducks and geese. Louisiana has always been a natural nesting ground, and a way stop on the great migration route that begins in South and Central America and goes northward to Canada. But we are losing much of the natural habitat to industry, the advance of the cities. We all should help when we can. These homes on stilts are artificial breeding places but when the trees become too crowded they will accept them. It's a small thing but it helps."

"I think it's a wonderful idea. Oh, look! There's a baby. Isn't he darling?"

They were beautiful birds, a pure white with black bills and legs and yellow feet. There was a great tumult on the platform; shifting for position, wing flapping, grooming, and parent birds coming and going feeding their young.

"Of course the egrets came so dangerously near extinction because of the demand for the plumes that appear on their backs during the mating season."

"Yes," she said, thinking of the silky white aigrette plumes adorning the heads of dowagers or the ceremonial head gear of Far Eastern potentates. The plumes seemed much more appropriate gleaming in the warm summer sun in their natural setting. Sherry could have watched for hours. In a few more minutes, however, Lucien started the motor, sending the colony into flapping panic for a moment, before he reversed slowly.

As they began to move there was a sudden disturbance in the water beneath the platform.

"What is that?" Sherry cried above the sound of their motor, pointing to where something long and thick roiled the water.

"An alligator," Lucien told her.

"Alligator?"

He nodded. "He's looking for food — fallen eggs, injured or crippled birds, overconfident nestlings fallen from the nest."

"If the egrets are so rare and the alligator preys upon them, why don't you kill it?"

He shook his head. "The alligator can't be blamed. He eats nothing, takes nothing, that would not be gone anyway. Nature has its checks and balances; the alligator is one of them. It keeps the colony healthy. Only the strong, the intelligent, and those in good health survive. It's cruel, perhaps, but effective."

It could not be denied and yet Sherry watched that log-like form in the water with hatred. She realized it was unfounded, still she could not help it. She shivered before she looked away and it was some minutes before she could shake off the depression that the sight of the alligator had brought.

They fished, they lay in the sun, talking little but feeling little real constraint here in the open air. Lucien cast for bass for a time, squinting into the rising sun, and Sherry sat watching him in a kind of lazy contentment. They cruised slowly along the bayou while Lucien pointed out a nutria swimming in the water. He showed her waterways clogged with floating mats of lavender-blue water hyacinths, a beautiful flower become a hazard to navigation. They saw clumps of ferns trailing their green swords among the black-green moss on the banks, and hanging curtains of orange trumpet vines running like fire among the trees. On the dryer stretches of ground palmetto clashed its tough leaves in the soft breeze.

A gull, inland from the gulf, shrilled its sharp cry above them. Families of ducks swam protesting out of their way. Along some of the meandering streams that ran together, trees meshed overhead providing a leafy tunnel down which they floated gently, their heads nearly touching the dripping moss.

It was, in its own way, a kind of paradise. A place filled with game and fish, where crops might be raised the year round, where a man if he put his mind to it need do little beyond seeing that food was on the table. Indolence seemed to be in the air, Sherry told herself, stretching lazily. Even she was affected.

Lunch was cold boiled shrimp, brought with them on ice, and French bread carefully wrapped in a pristine white napkin. To drink there was beer or tea, both icy cold, and for dessert there were fresh, tree ripened peaches to eat with a chilled white wine.

They lay propped on the boat seats, peeling shrimp, dipping them into a hot, tart sauce and popping them into their mouths. It seemed enough to enjoy the food and the sense of lazy companionship without questioning what would follow. Deep inside, Sherry did not trust the man beside her in this mood, could not believe that it would last. When he turned to her suddenly she jumped and had to control an urge to move away, out of his reach.

"How do you feel now?" he asked her. "Less like a prisoner?"

"It's been a lovely morning," she told him with real gratitude. "I've enjoyed it so much."

"There will be others," he said, "now that all is safe and no one is going to send out a search party on your behalf. There will be many days ahead to savor. There is no need to rush like a glutton to the feast. We could go out into the gulf. You would be able to swim there in the cleaner salt water and lie on the sandy beaches."

"That would be nice," she replied, conscious that her answer sounded like a child's who has been promised a treat it knew it should be thankful for.

"I don't suppose it sounds all that exciting, but there is a limit to the entertainment to be found at Bayou's End. Of course if you prefer lying reading at the big house—"

"No," she said hastily. "I'll be glad to go."

At least the outings in the boat would remove her from the house and Marie's silent uncommunicative presence.

"What is it?" he asked, annoyance in his voice. "Is my company so repugnant or is it that you would rather find your own amusement?"

It was useless to try to deceive him, Sherry thought, and she refused to pretend any longer or to hide her feelings in an attempt to influence him. She didn't care what he thought of her.

"I didn't ask for your company," she told him. "However, since there's no help for it I can bear it. But I would like to be asked. No woman likes to be ordered about."

"And if I had asked you — what would you have said?"

"I'd have said thank you very nicely and left the outing arrangements to you, since I didn't know what Bayou's End has by the way of entertainment."

"You see? You would have carefully placed the burden of decision back in my lap. Which only proves women enjoy being dictated to, otherwise they would not invite it so often."

"Not necessarily. There is a great deal of difference between being a leader and being a dictator," she told him with asperity. "Women have no more liking for domineering, over-bearing men who gloat in their power than does another man." She looked away gathering her thoughts. "Between any two people, one usually has greater strength or a more commanding personality than the other, regardless of whether they are the same sex or not. Insofar as it is possible, however, men and women should be equal in their relationship, two parts of a whole. Men and women have complementing roles. Neither one exploits the other. They each have a job that must be done to raise their family and make life livable. And if in their relationship the man is stronger, a woman can and will accept this and enjoy it. But only if he uses his strength, and the authority that it gives him, with love."

He stared at her, his eyes narrowed into unreadable slits. "You seem to have given a lot of thought to your philosophy."

"What woman hasn't, these days?"

"And yet I wonder if, like most of us, you haven't said more than you intended? Never mind. Come, *Chérie,* I would enjoy your company very much if you will let me take you out in this next few days."

She smiled and agreed, lulled by the pleasantly worded plea. A moment later she frowned. Had she, by her agreement altered her status with Lucien? Didn't her acceptance of his company and his plans for her entertainment make her seem a willing party to her abduction, at least when they were away from the house? It could not be helped. Every prisoner had to make some accommodation to circumstances; the trick was in knowing where to draw the line.

The heat of the day was upon them and they headed home as soon as the lunch hamper and ice chest had been packed away. Sherry, wrapped in her own misgivings, did not speak as they sped along, and Lucien concentrated to the exclusion of all else on the piloting of the boat along the twisting course.

Once they passed another boat with a man fishing, half hidden in the shadows of the overhang of a large water oak. The man lifted his hand, but either Lucien did not see him or he did not want to acknowledge the greeting.

Sherry glanced at Lucien, then she looked away. What difference did it make to her that he had snubbed a friend?

And so the time passed, merging into one long summer day filled with the glitter of the black waters of the bayou and also the liquid aquamarine of the gulf, of sand and swimming and fishing, quick tropical storms and fierce sun, and Lucien in anger, but also in easy camaraderie. In that time – though he seemed to find satisfaction in forcing her to accept his kiss when they met and parted – at night she slept undisturbed.

Once, as they rocked gently on the turquoise waves of the gulf in the cabin cruiser, Sherry had gone forward to lie on the deck, soaking up the sun. After a few minutes she heard Lucien approach. He lowered himself to the hot fiberglass sheeting nearby, though he did not speak.

Through slitted eyes Sherry studied him; his brooding face with its heavy brows and thick lashes, the crisp waves of his hair, and his wide, muscled shoulders washed by the golden light of the semitropical sun. An ache grew in her chest, spreading upward to her throat. A vast depression seized her and she felt the rise of tears, senseless tears she was unable to explain.

In that instant Lucien turned his head. Sherry let her eyes close, willing her lashes to lie still. She could sense his gaze upon her, yet she was unprepared for the touch of his hand on her shoulder.

Her eyes flew open and she stared straight

up into his. For one unguarded moment she thought she saw a dark reflection of her own pain there, then as he spoke it was gone.

"Time to turn," he said. "Don't fall asleep; the sun will burn you before you realize it this time of year."

With a nod, she obeyed the suggestion. She turned her face away from the man beside her. Swallowing against the tightness in her throat, she forced herself to analyze the feeling that gripped her. She was not homesick. Paul's disappointment in her did not make her that unhappy. She no longer felt despair at her situation, or even real mistrust of Lucien's motives. It was some time before she could bring herself to acknowledge the reason for her distress, though the answer was simple. It was regret.

10

One evening as they sat on the gallery after dinner a small boat putt-putted up the bayou and drew into the shore beside the steps of the wooden dock. A family of seven piled out, from toddlers to teenagers, including what was apparently the mother and father.

Lucien got to his feet to walk to the top of the steps just as the older man, in the lead, called out a greeting.

"Hey, Lucien! You blind, man? You pass me say three – four days ago on the bayou. You not even see me, man. Got eyes for no one but that girl standing up there with you, I know, me. She's some looker, *n'est-ce pas?* You done shocked ten years off Mama's life."

"That's for true, *cher!*" his wife agreed. "When Papa told me you had a beautiful blonde with you here I couldn't believe my ears."

"Come in, come in," Lucien cut across the woman's voice somewhat hurriedly. "Let me introduce you, Sherry, to Mama and Papa Arceneaux, Lottie and Toto. They are true Cajuns, descendants of the French Acadians who migrated to Louisiana from Nova Scotia two hundred years ago, give or take a year."

Sherry shook hands with the couple. Short in stature, they both had dark hair and flashing black eyes in weathered faces. Their easy manners and good-natured smiles made them easy to like. The children, a well-mannered group, were the image of their parents. Lottie introduced them one by one, before waving her brood to a sitting place on the steps. She and her husband drew up chairs, pulling them close to those of Sherry and Lucien for a cozy grouping.

Lucien excused himself in order to tell Marie to bring refreshments. When he had gone Lottie turned to Sherry.

"When did you two get married? I am some mad, me, that I didn't get an invitation to the wedding. I've known that Lucien since we were kids, and I'm going to give him a piece of my mind for keeping so quiet about you."

"We — aren't married." Sherry answered,

embarrassment making her speak more shortly than she had intended. They were his friends; let him explain. Still, as silence met her words, she felt a flush mounting under her skin and she found herself wishing he would hurry back.

Lottie was equal to the occasion, however. "Not married? You hear that, Papa? We're not too late for the wedding."

"Oh, n—nothing is settled yet," Sherry stammered. She could not allow Lottie to continue in that vein and have Lucien think she had told his friends they were to be married. On the other hand, she could not bring herself to tell the woman flatly that there was no possibility of it, not while she and Lucien were so obviously spending some time together here at his bayou retreat.

"Ah? Not to worry. I am thinking it will not be long." She gave Sherry a conspiratorial wink as the sound of Lucien's footsteps signaled his return.

It was nice to feel that Lottie was on her side. The feeling of instant rapport was so great Sherry was able to relax and summon a smile, secure in the knowledge that Lottie Arceneaux would say nothing to embarrass her.

Lucien glanced at Sherry as he took his seat

once more. Seeing the high color just fading from her cheeks, he lifted a quizzical brow, his gaze going from Sherry to his guests. Lottie gave him a bland smile.

"Women talk," snorted Lottie's husband. "But I was wanting to see that new boat you got down there, me."

Leaving Sherry and Lottie in comfort on the gallery, the two men strolled down the steps toward the dock. Most of the children followed, skipping and laughing behind them. One of them, a baby boy of about two, with fat legs, great brown eyes, and a melting smile, got halfway down the slope when he suddenly sat down. His dignity injured, he set up a howl. Lucien turned and swung the child up onto his shoulders with a few words in his deep voice. Miraculously, the crying ceased. The baby laughed, catching a handful of Lucien's hair as a handhold as they continued on their way.

Involuntarily the corners of Sherry's mouth curved in a smile at the picture.

"You like the *bébé?*" Lottie said. "That is good. So many girls these days want only one, maybe two *bébés*. What kind of family is that, hah? I ask you? So selfish. Who the little ones going to play with? They have nobody, 'cept maybe Mama and Daddy, and they off working. And don't tell me about no population explosion. That's thinking in cold blood, almost as bad as love in cold blood."

Sherry laughed at the droll look on Lottie's face. Here in this fecund climate with its wealth of natural riches it did seem a shame to be so stingy with children, to follow any other than nature's laws. And yet, if she followed the prompting of nature— She thrust the thought from her, dragging her eyes from Lucien's tall form.

"Do you live nearby?" she asked Lottie.

"Oh, a few miles down the bayou."

"You live here all year round?"

"Sure. We have a little house and a patch of land. In the summer my Toto goes out with the shrimp trawlers and in the winter there's his trap line. It's a good life."

"Don't you miss having neighbors?"

"Neighbors? We got neighbors. There's a dozen, two dozen families on the bayous, not far. Most of them connected kin, you understand?"

"Oh? I had the idea the bayou was almost deserted. We saw no sign of houses the other day."

"Now that Lucien, maybe he not want any company, hah?" Lottie gave a rich laugh, her eyes sparkling with a teasing amusement.

"There's always friends, neighbors. Course there's ways of avoiding friends too. Plenty of back bayous, little streams fit only for navigation by nutshells — though most bayou men's boats will run on a heavy dew, or so they'll tell you, even that fancy rig of Lucien's out there. But maybe I'd better call my kids and my Toto? Maybe you not wanting company either?"

"Oh, no — no," Sherry exclaimed. "I'm glad you came."

Lottie turned shrewd eyes on her, a still expression on her face. "Men can be a trouble, can't they? Just remember they are human, just like us." She nodded emphatically. "Now you, how you like to go to a party?"

"A party?"

"Sure. Why not? A real old-fashioned *fais-do-do*. You have heard of it?"

"No, I can't say I have."

"It means stay-up-all-night. Everybody come, *Grand'mére*, *Grand'pére*, *Tante*, *'Nonc*, all the children. We eat, drink, dance to the fiddles. Everything is all planned. You just got to bring yourselves."

"It sounds like fun." Sherry answered. "But I'm not sure—"

"You mean you think maybe Lucien won't come? Then you don't know Lucien. He's been to many a *fais-do-do,* not so much in the last years, but when he was younger."

"I couldn't answer for him."

"Then ask him. He won't tell me no, you'll see." Glancing toward the dock, she saw the men returning. "Hey you, Lucien!" she called. "You want to *fais-do-do?*"

The dark man with the child still on his shoulders did not answer, turning instead to Toto. The two women could see them talking as they advanced. They climbed the steps and sat down beside Lottie and Sherry, Lucien joggling the child on his knee. Sherry watched them, a strange feeling in her chest.

Finally Lucien glanced up at Lottie. "I don't think—" he began.

"Come, Lucien. Your *Chérie* wants to go. She has never been to one before. It will be an experience for her."

"I don't doubt it," he told her, the teeth flashing in his face. "But what kind? Are you certain she would appreciate it?"

"Oh yes, Lucien I can tell, me. Don't be so without grace, man. You come, you leave early. You don't have to stay up all night, just until after the jumping of the broom. My oldest sister's girl, Sophia, she wants to keep the tradition. She—"

They were interrupted by Marie bringing

212

coffee and cake, and ice cream for the children. The housekeeper stayed a few moments to greet the Arceneaux family and exchange a few words. When she had gone, Lucien, who had been studying Sherry's face, her careful composure and the downsweep of her lashes, slowly nodded. "Yes, we will come," he said.

"Ah, good." Lottie sighed as if greatly relieved. "Tomorrow night. You come about dark, leave at daylight or whenever you take the notion."

They went to the *fais-do-do* by water, of course. Sherry would have liked to sit with Lucien outside at the controls in the fresh night air. He discouraged her. Her hair would be windblown, he said, and her white dress in danger of coming in contact with oil and grease, or the sweep of overhanging branches. She rode in lonely state in the cabin.

The dress of white eyelet had not been her idea. Lucien had suggested it when she asked his advice on what would be suitable. It was the same dress she had worn to dinner her first night at Bayou's End, not an occasion of pleasant memories for either of them, she was sure. Why he had chosen it, she could not imagine. She had considered refusing to wear it. She did not know why she had agreed, unless it was some element of taut control in his face. There had been something different about him since yesterday afternoon, something she could not quite define to her satisfaction.

Though it was growing late, the afterglow still lingered in the sky and she could see the interior of the boat around her. She stared at her hands, playing with a crease of her dress.

She could almost believe that Lucien had enjoyed her company the last few days. For herself, the world of Bayou's End had absorbed her. She had grown so used to it, to her strange place in it, that it seemed reality, and the life she had left the dream, with Paul but a shadowy figure in it. She did not understand herself. She no longer felt threatened. A sense of inevitability was upon her, lulling her, sapping her will to resist.

Her thoughts were so deep that she scarcely noticed the time or the distance they had traveled. She was startled to hear the boat's motors change as they glided into the landing at the Arceneaux's house.

Lucien gave her his hand up from the cabin. She stepped out onto the deck into a dusk darkness lit by bobbing owl-shaped lanterns, many of them dancing over their reflections in the bayou.

The house, a rambling, gray, one-story structure with cypress shingles and a long front gallery, looked as though it had been added to at random over the years. It was set back from the bayou with strings of colored lights running from the trees near the landing to its four corners. Lights also decorated the open-air pavilion for dancing that had been constructed nearer the bayou. It was a platform built close to the ground with four stout corner posts to hold the lights, and a small raised dais to one side for the musicians. It was garlanded with crepe paper streamers and forest greenery that lent a fresh woodsy scent to the atmosphere.

Boats of all descriptions were pulled up on the banks and tied to the shaky dock, for a large crowd had already gathered. Laughing groups of people stood about, most of them with something to eat or drink in their hands. Children ran here and there, ducking and dodging among their elders. The scene had the feel of a picnic or a family reunion.

The Arceneaux boat dock was lower than the one at Bayou's End so that the deck of the cruiser was slightly above it. Lucien jumped to the planking, then reached up to swing her down beside him. As he encircled her with his arm, leading her toward the house and the people that moved to greet them, she thought there was something possessive in his clasp upon her waist. She glanced up at him, but his face was set in grim, unreadable lines. Even the appearance of Lottie, coming toward them with a gay hail, did not have the power to make him relax, though his mouth curved in a smile.

"Ah, *cher*," Lottie cried. "I am so happy to see you both. Will you have something to eat, boiled shrimp, some gumbo, something?"

"We have already had dinner," Lucien told her.

"Now why did you do that? You know there is always food for all at a *fais-do-do*. Come, anyway, and have something to drink. My Toto is barman tonight. He will fix you up."

They were drawn into the laughing, chattering crowd. Dozens of people were introduced to her, Aunt this, Uncle that, cousins, nieces, and nephews; so many so quickly that it was impossible to remember all the names. A glass was pressed into her hand, a concoction of fruit juices laced lightly with rum. In the fresh evening air, with the warm press of humanity, her throat felt dry and she drank thirstily only to have her glass refilled.

As the evening advanced, and Lucien gave her yet another fresh glass, she slanted him a wary look. The mixture in her glass seemed innocuous enough but she was aware of her limitations. She was not used to anything much stronger than wine, and she certainly had no intention of allowing herself to become befuddled.

"Don't be so suspicious," he murmured, his lips against the softness of her hair. She found herself smiling, reassured.

She was introduced to a number of women around the dessert table, several of them with young children. They began to ask her about her home. Seeing her in good hands, Lucien left her. Glancing about a few minutes later, she saw him talking to Lottie, their heads close together and their faces intent. Again a sense of disquiet assailed her, but at that moment Lucien looked up and, catching her gaze, sent her a grin. She felt her own lips curving and chided herself silently for being so nervous.

As Lucien returned to her side, there was a general surge toward the pavilion platform. They joined the crowd gathering to watch the fiddlers and the accordionist tune up. Then the musicians, each man with a drink at his elbow, began to play. It was the lilting, foot-tapping music of the bayous.

There was no reluctance, no hesitation at

being the first one out on the floor. Suddenly the open space was filled with dancing couples, their eyes shining with the pleasure of the rhythm and the uninhibited enjoyment of moving in time to the music.

Sherry could feel an eagerness to join them rising within her. Lucien stood back, however, seemingly content to watch. She saw one or two men cast speculative glances at her, then turn to find their partners. Was it because of the man at her side and her ambiguous position as the only guest at his house that they hesitated to approach her? Perhaps the gossip had already spread? It would not be surprising in a closeknit society such as this. No, Lottie would not gossip about them. What was it, then, that set Lucien and herself apart? The only other couple left so isolated was Lottie's niece Sophie and the young man who had been introduced as her fiancée.

Frowning, Sherry flicked a glance at her escort. His attention caught, he leaned closer to be heard over the music. "What is it? Is something wrong?"

"I—everyone looks at us so strangely. I don't think we quite fit in," she told him.

"No, not quite. We are dry-landers most of the time, both of us. Don't let it bother you.

Relax and enjoy yourself. This night will never come again."

As if reminded of his duty, he drew her out onto the floor. She tried to do as he had suggested, giving herself to the music and the sensation of being in his arms with the gaiety and laughter around them. The music was fast, a cross between a polka and a fox-trot, galloping music that demanded a tight grip on your partner; music with no patience for its modern counterpart where partners were often separated by the width of the room.

Ya-hoo! The Cajun call echoed on the air, a sign of enjoyment. The music went on and on as the men on the dais switched effortlessly from one tune to another. Shoes were kicked off, hairpins were lost, feet and elbows flew. As the floor became crowded it became a game to keep time to the music and, at the same time, keep from bumping into other couples. Several times she was pulled tightly against Lucien's chest, and his warm breath fanned her cheeks as he grinned down at her. It was great and hilarious fun. Sherry, when at last the music stopped, was laughing and breathless. A drink seemed in order for their dry throats, and then, as the musicians struck up again, she and Lucien stood with their glasses in their hands, watching the dancers and commenting on them. It seemed to Sherry that something of the tension between them was gone, dissolved in the closeness of the dance.

The moon rose in splendor, an isolated, cool ball beyond the glow of the lanterns. Sherry called Lucien's attention to it as it glimmered ghostlike above the tops of the trees. It was growing late. The children had been put to bed on pallets in one of the spare rooms of the house with some of the older women to keep watch. Still the music went on and on as if it would never end and the Cajuns matched it with a fine abandon. Fathers danced with teenage daughters, mothers with sons, nephews with aunts, and brothers with sisters. Over to one side, beneath a lantern suspended from a tree limb, some of the older men had begun a card game. Occasionally, a man would come up to Lucien and they would talk in quiet voices for a time. Sometimes their wives would come to speak a few words to Sherry, but when she was left alone she could not help overhearing the conversations beside her. Most of the men, it seemed, wanted advice about their problems, problems that concerned the shrimping industry, the trapping grounds available and which was best; or sometimes it was a job on one of the offshore oil rigs, or on a ship, that was sought.

She and Lucien danced once or twice more as the crowds began to thin. Whether it was fact or imagination, she began to think that there was constraint on the spirits of these bayou people while they were on the floor. Then, as they stood near the edge of the outdoor pavilion, she noticed that no one crowded near them. It occurred to her to wonder if it was respect, rather than mere good manners or distrust, that caused these people to leave them to themselves. She found herself looking at Lucien from a new angle. Why should these people look up to him? Was it because he was so obviously rich and influential, so that they expected him to know more about what went on in the outside world? Was it his ancient family, the lasting effects of the patron system? Or was it something within the man himself that caused them to rely on his judgment?

At last the moon began to wane. As the energy of the dancers lagged, Toto walked to the center of the floor and held up his hands for silence. "Mesdames, Messieurs, we have the treat tonight, the great treat! We have for you the ceremony of the jumping of the broom. Not in, maybe, ten years have we seen it, but tonight we have two couples!"

A fanfare rose from the musicians. With a buzz of excitement, the crowd drew back to form a circle around the edge of the platform, leaving the center and one end open.

Lucien caught Sherry's elbow, leading her back to the edge of the crowd.

"Will the *fais-do-do* be finished when this is over?" she whispered.

He nodded and descended the back steps of the pavilion, then began to circle the edge.

"Where are we going?" she asked, thinking that perhaps Lucien had seen a better vantage point.

He did not answer immediately. They stopped near another couple just out of the range of the lights. Glancing at them, Sherry saw that it was Sophia and her fiancée. She smiled at the girl in her long dress of white voile, almost like a wedding dress. She was young, a teenager with shy eyes and long fine lashes, and with her dark hair falling in ringlets from the crown of her head. The boy beside her was dark and on the stocky side, but the look in his eyes was tender as he smiled at the girl beside him.

"Are you going to jump the broom too?" the girl spoke to Sherry, her English less accented than that of most of the older people.

She began to shake her head when Lucien answered for her.

"Yes," he said.

"But I don't—"

Lucien leaned close, speaking softly for her ear alone. "It's only a game, a romantic tradition. Humor them, please, *Chérie.* For my sake."

Lucien did not speak again, but stood holding her eyes with his own, willing her to do as he asked. A hush was gradually descending upon the crowd, a hush filled with a growing expectancy.

Sherry thought there was a promise she could not understand in Lucien's black, fathomless gaze. She felt detached, and yet as though she were on the brink of something important.

"Lucien—" she whispered. He would not help her; she saw that without understanding it. Though the outcome mattered greatly to him, he would not force her decision. She was free to give the answer that would please him, or to refuse in an exercise of spite. Suddenly she smiled. "All right," she said, and turned to face the crowd.

"Sophia and her fiancée will go first. Just do as they do," Lucien told her. He drew her hand through his arm, covered it with his own and stood waiting.

A soft, haunting melody began to rise from the accordion. A new broom with a white handle decorated with silver knots of ribbon appeared magically, and Toto, with another man Sherry recognized vaguely as his brother, stepped forward to hold it a few inches from the floor.

The young couple ahead of them smiled at each other, then, holding hands, they moved slowly forward to the music and leaped lightly over the broom.

A murmur ran over the crowd, then died away, as the couple took up a stance on one side.

Lucien caught Sherry's hand and drew her forward. The broom was before her. She saw Lottie watching and caught Toto's grin. Then she was over.

11

Cheers burst from all sides and people gathered around them. Toto shook Lucien's hand. "I am a witness, me, and there are any number who will swear they saw you too. Well done, Sherry," he said, beaming at her, giving her name the same sound of an endearment that Lucien did.

Champagne was broached and a toast was drunk to each couple and to their happiness. Sherry's head began to ache with the babble of strange voices and the confusion that rushed in upon her as she received what seemed to be an excess of congratulations for the smallness of her feat. The chatter seemed to reverberate in her ears, and the press of people around her was suffocating. She clung to Lucien's arm with a grip that left the ends of her fingers white.

Lucien glanced down at her. "Shall we go?" he whispered. At her nod and strained smile, he began to make their excuses, moving purposefully out of the press. Their way was blocked for a moment by an old woman dressed in rusty black with a scarf thrown over her head. As she muttered and made the sign of the cross in the air, the talking and laughter ceased. Sherry looked up at Lucien, her eyes wide and imploring.

"It's only a blessing," he murmured. With unexpected courtesy he thanked the wizened yet dignified old crone. She nodded, her face creasing in a smile, before she stepped back into the crowd.

The trip back to Bayou's End was swift. Sherry stood beside Lucien, letting the cool breeze of their passage clear her head and banish the cobwebs that clung to her mind. She went back over the evening step by step, gradually recapturing some of her earlier enjoyment. Still, the ceremony at the last disturbed her thoughts. It was not until they had reached their own dock and left the boat and the noisy roar of its motor that she asked Lucien to explain what the jumping of the broom meant.

They walked on and she seemed to sense a rare indecision in his silence. At last he sighed, staring at the house before them.

"I told you, *Chérie*. It was only a game."

She considered that, measuring it against what she felt as much as what she knew. It did not satisfy her. The problem did not seem important enough for further discussion, however. She was so tired, and acceptance was easier than argument.

She whispered, "All right, Lucien."

He turned to her, drawing her into his arms with a tenderness that breached her defenses much more effectively than forceful passion could ever have done. She felt herself yielding, swaying against him. His lips burned on hers, setting the blood to racing in her veins. He touched her cheek with gentle fingers, then trailed down the creamy curve of her neck to the low neck of her bodice.

A warning echoed in Sherry's mind, but as his kiss deepened and his firm sure touch brought its response, the will to heed it grew faint. She felt herself pressed close, so close her body seemed almost to merge with his and was yet not close enough.

"Lucien," she whispered, a sound half plea, half protest as he lowered his head to brush a warm caress across the curve of her breasts exposed by her neckline.

For an endless stretch of time he was still.

The only sound in the strained quiet was the soft rasp of their breathing.

Without warning he lifted her into his arms and carried her up the steps and across the dim gallery lit only by the iron lantern. At the door of her room he twisted the knob and kicked the panel open, striding toward the large tester bed. The still blackness of the room was around them. She felt his arms tighten, the muscles cording to the tension and strength of steel. He drew a deep breath, holding it constricted in his chest.

Sherry lay unmoving. The strong beat of his heart was echoed in her own bloodstream, along with a breathless apprehension.

Once more she felt the sensuous fire of his mouth on hers, then he lowered her to the bed, pressed a kiss to each eyelid and left her.

She turned over, hiding her face in her pillow as hot tears slid from her eyes, tears of relief, she told herself. But if that was so, why did they have the feel of despair?

She awoke stiff and cold, with the sound of a boat's motor thrumming in the back of her mind. The room was dim, filled with the underwater murkiness of a cloudy dawn. Her eyes burned behind her tangled lashes and she put her hands up to them, pressing against their ache.

It was early for visitors, she thought. It could be that Lucien was leaving, except that she was almost sure the sound had been coming toward the house, not moving away from it.

Memories of the night before slid into the forefront of her mind, but she banished them fiercely, deliberately making her mind a blank. She would not think.

She sat up on the edge of the bed, trying to find the strength to get up, to wash her face and change from the white dress she still wore into a nightgown before going back to bed. Abruptly she went still. She heard voices coming from out on the gallery. Paul. It was Paul!

She jumped up, moving toward the door. Halfway across the room she stopped. She could not let Paul see her like this, in the evening dress she had worn the night before, with stale makeup on her face, her pale mouth vulnerable without lipstick, and her eyes shadowed from crying. What would he think? He could not be blamed if he suspected Lucien of mistreating her. That she could not allow.

Swinging around, she reached back to unzip

her dress. In the haste of the moment, the zipper jammed and precious seconds were wasted getting it unstuck.

She showered quickly, donned a sundress of apple green, and brushed her hair to shining smoothness. She took longer than usual over her makeup to eradicate all traces of her distress. As she worked, her mind was with the two men outside. What was happening between Lucien and his brother? Was Lucien telling Paul about her being here? How would he explain it, or would he even try? If Lucien chose to be difficult, would she be able to convince Paul that she was not here of her own free will? And if he believed her, what then? How would it affect his feelings toward his brother?

Paul might not be in love with her, still he was unlikely to take her abduction by Lucien calmly. So far there had been no sound of voices raised in anger. If only it stayed that way!

A last touch of lip gel and she was ready. All was still quiet on the gallery. An uneasy thought assailed her. Surely Lucien would tell Paul? He could not leave it for her to walk out upon him unprepared!

An instant later the dismay caused by this possibility was driven from her mind as if it had never been. It was ousted by a sound, a roaring noise that grew louder, the noise of boat engines. With the pot of lip gel in her hand, Sherry stood listening, staring at her reflection in the mirror in stunned disbelief. Paul was leaving!

Sherry set the gel down with a clatter, crossed the room, and flung open the door. Stepping to the edge of the gallery, she clung to one of the colonnettes. In the murky light of the morning she could see the two cruisers on the lake, both moving toward the bayou. The one in the lead was already fast disappearing behind the screening branches of the trees.

"Paul!" she cried, though she knew it would do no good. She could not be heard above the sound of the motors. The second boat, with Lucien at the wheel, wallowed in the over-deep wake of the first. He did not look back as it moved out of sight also. The stuttering echo died away and quiet returned.

Her face pale, Sherry turned away. She sank down into one of the cushioned rattan chairs, resting her head against its high back. How Lucien must be laughing! He had won again. Today was Saturday, the date of the party for Aimee. No doubt that was why Paul had come, to make certain his brother meant to attend. And so Lucien had departed in the early-morning coolness, leaving her alone. Soon, however, the gala would be over. What then? Would Lucien return to his docile prisoner? Would they go on as before, until the novelty of the arrangement palled for him, or would it be over when next his boat came into sight?

Her hands, lying along the arms of her chair, clenched into fists. A haunted look in her eyes, she stared out over the lawn, watching without seeing the green darkness gathering under the oaks. Distant thunder rumbled, a threatening sound. Rain began to fall in a drifting mist.

"Pardon?"

The quiet voice belonged to Marie. Sherry looked up to see the housekeeper standing beside her with a breakfast tray in her hands. She greeted her with a wan smile and, at a gesture, reached to draw a small table in front of her chair. The housekeeper set the tray in place, then brought an extra cushion to tuck behind Sherry's back. Her smile was soft, almost maternal, and Sherry glanced at her from the corners of her eyes, thinking that Marie was as given to moods lately as she was herself.

The tray was lovely; it was easy to see

Marie had gone to a great deal of trouble. Of rattan and bamboo, it was covered with a tray cloth of pink linen. On the cloth rested a place setting of the same ancient china and glassware that had graced the table that first night, and lying in one corner was a perfect double pink hibiscus flower in full bloom. A linen napkin held several hot crusty rolls and there was also butter molded in the shape of daisies, and a tiny, individual coffeepot.

Sherry thanked Marie and complimented her on the tray, hoping that she would understand the tone if not the words.

Marie nodded, satisfied, and went away on quiet feet, a gleam of some secret amusement shining in her eyes.

Because Marie had gone to so much trouble, Sherry made an effort to eat the breakfast. She sipped the hot, delicious coffee, and the rolls she could not eat she crumbled and threw to a pair of squabbling sparrows fluttering about in the softly falling rain.

In a little while Marie removed the tray and as they smiled silently, Sherry wished that she could communicate with her. Someone to talk to, on a gray day like today when Lucien was away and she was cut off from everyone, would have made so much difference. Today she felt like a prisoner, more so than at any moment since Lucien had carried her from his boat.

Her depression was so great that it was with genuine pleasure that the sound of a motor brought her upright in her chair. Within seconds the realization came that it could not be Lucien. The throbbing noise was too faint, too slow, for his powerful cruiser. The boat, when it finally came into view, was a wooden skiff powered by an ancient outboard motor. With some slight lifting of her depression Sherry recognized its sole occupant under the camouflaging of yellow rain gear and a man's old felt hat. It was Lottie.

The boat drew into the dock. As the Cajun woman climbed out and started up the wet, grassy slope, Sherry got to her feet and went down the steps to meet her.

"Ah, *Chérie*! How are you this morning?" Lottie called as soon as she was in earshot. "Just as I thought. You are looking sad. I have come to cheer you. Not that I blame you, mind. It is a sad day when a honeymoon must be interrupted! I could not believe my eyes when I saw the boats go by this morning. I did not see you beside Lucien and so I thought to me, she is all alone. He will be gone all day for sure and it is bad to be left alone now, even if the homecoming is sweet."

Sherry hardly heard what she said. Her mind had stopped.

"H—honeymoon?" she stammered.

"But of course! *Chérie,* do you feel all right? You are as white as the sheet."

Sherry reached out and caught the other woman's arm. "Whose honeymoon?"

"Why, yours, *Chérie,* and that of Lucien!" Lottie's face changed. "You do not know? But you must — you jumped the broom!"

"I—exactly what does this jumping the broom mean?"

"That you are married — to Lucien."

"Married! I can't be. I don't believe it!"

A grim look came into Lottie's eyes. "Did Lucien not tell you?" she said. "That is bad, very bad."

"I don't understand. How can I be married?" Sherry pressed trembling fingers to her temples as she tried to comprehend.

"It is an old tradition here in the bayou country. It goes back to the old times when the colonies were new. A man and woman in those days were long weary miles from the church or a priest, and nature, *Chérie,* does not like to wait. To jump the broom together before witnesses was the same as exchanging the sacred vows, a promise made each to the other and strengthened by the blessing of an old one such as *Grand'mère* Lelia, who wished for you and Lucien joy following every sorrow and many children." Lottie gave a tiny shrug though her face mirrored her distress for Sherry's ignorance.

"I can't believe it," Sherry whispered.

"Nor I," Lottie agreed. "It is not like Lucien to mock the traditions of the bayou. There must be a reason."

"Never mind the reasons," Sherry said with a shake of her head. She thought she knew them. "This ceremony can't be legal, can it?"

"The custom has been recognized for over two hundred years in this part of the state. It is not done so much today, but the old ways of doing things die hard. For my niece Sophia and her young man there will be another wedding before the priest." Lottie went on, her voice suddenly practical. "I tell you what I would do. Lucien Villeré is much of a man; it would be foolish to let him go. If I were you, I would get him before the priest without delay. There is nothing like the words of the good father, and two marriages are little enough to hold the man you have jumped the broom with. That is, if you want to hold him."

The idea was ridiculous. Of course she did not want to hold him, and yet how could she say so, after spending this week with Lucien, without appearing immoral? Moreover, although she might not have to associate with these people again, Lucien would. How could she destroy their simple faith in him and the respect in which he was held? She forced her stiff lips into a smile. "I'm not sure what I want."

"It is natural to be angry with Lucien," Lottie said, her sunny nature asserting itself once more. "I would be myself, in your place. But only think what a romantic gesture it was, what a fine surprise!"

"Yes, it was certainly a surprise," Sherry agreed.

"Lucien will not like it that I have told you. It will serve him right though for leaving it until the morning, and for going off to New Orleans without you. Maybe it would be better if you don't tell him I let the cat out. He will enjoy his surprise so much more. Men, eh?" The Cajun woman's mouth quirked in a grin.

Sherry cast about in her mind for a change of subject. "You saw the boat that came for Lucien this morning, I think you said. Do you know who owns it?"

"It was a boat much like Lucien's, I think, me, it belongs to his brother, Paul Villeré."

"I see," Sherry said quietly. There was no hope of a mistake then.

Lottie shrugged out of her raincoat and left it to drip on the newel of the stair banister. Before they had settled into their chairs, Marie appeared with coffee and cake. As Sherry lifted her cup she glanced out across the side lawn, her attention caught by a flicker of movement.

It was Jules, weighted with fishing tackle, making for the boat house. Apparently he no longer feared that she would try to leave, no longer felt it necessary to guard her. He knew then, and Marie also. That explained the woman's change. Sherry had her approval now that she was the master's wife. Wife. She couldn't be. She couldn't.

She settled down to try to behave as normally as possible. She was even able to joke in mock anger of the revenge she would have upon Lucien for leading her into such an alliance.But though she chattered with a forced gaiety for the length of Lottie's visit, the words that rang in her head as she saw the Cajun woman off in her boat at the dock were Lucien's. Only a game, he had said. *Only a game.*

She thought of the moment beneath the trees when she had asked Lucien to explain to her what he had meant. Why hadn't she questioned him further? Why hadn't she demanded to know the significance of the jumping of the broom? Was it because she had sensed even then that she would not like the answer?

She had been tricked; there was no other word for it. The purpose was not hard to see. If she and Paul had really been engaged, her position would now be impossible. Not only had it been made to appear that she had gone away willingly with Lucien, but it must also look as though she had grasped at the flimsiest of excuses to tie him to her, forgetting her supposed fiancée as if he did not exist. It did not make a pretty picture. Further, if in her anger she should decide to try pressing formal charges against Lucien, her public appearance with him could be used to make her seem a liar and a fool.

And yet, it did not make sense. If this ceremony did in fact have a legal basis, then why would Lucien bind himself to her? To go through a marriage with her, however informal the ceremony may have been, was a ridiculous length to go just to prevent his brother from doing the same thing.

An annulment. Considering Lucien's behavior the night before, their wedding night if Lottie were to be believed, it seemed likely that a course of action was in his mind. Still, would such legal means be necessary? Was there in truth any legal basis for this so-called marriage? She could not, she would not, believe it. And even if there were, she refused to be bound by a custom she had never heard of until a few hours ago, and still did not fully understand. Nor would she stay here meekly waiting for Lucien to return and dispose of her at his convenience like some unwanted parcel.

She swung around, staring after Lottie. How stupid she was. If only she had thought to ask if she could go with her. There might have been someone she could hire to take her back to New Orleans. Now it was too late, Lottie was gone. The lake was still once more. The rain had died away, leaving the surface of the water as smooth and gray as polished steel. The only movement was on the far edge where Jules sat in his drifting boat casting for bass.

There had to be some other means of escape; the only problem was finding it. With luck, she should have twenty-four hours to go about it. There was at least one thing in her favor there had never been before — Jules and Marie's lack of vigilance. Irresistibly, her considering was drawn once more to the boat on the lake.

A gust of wind swept across the gallery, ruffling Sherry's hair, blowing long strands across her face. Its momentary coolness made her realize how sultry the air had become. The humidity was so oppressive it was hard to breathe. In the southeast was a towering bank of clouds that seemed to be moving with ominous swiftness toward them. Even as she watched, the light began to change, darkening, taking on a sulfurous tint. From the far end of the lake rose an enormous flock of snowy egrets. They swirled higher, as if caught in an updraft, an aerial whirlpool of white birds. Lining out, they flew inland, the beat of their long wings like muffled applause. Hard on their heels was a group of sea gulls. Their breasts were touched with yellow from the peculiar light as they skimmed the tops of the trees, shrieking their displeasure with the high wind that drove them.

Out on the lake, Jules cranked his motor and sent his boat toward shore. The surface of the lake, smooth an instant before, was now choppy with waves, and the lightweight aluminum craft skimmed over them scattering spray and white flecks of foam. To the south, the trees that ringed the horizon were suddenly blotted out by a dragging gray curtain of rain.

Ignoring the dock, Jules ran the boat up to the bank, jumped out and pulled it up halfway out of the lake. Leaving it, he made for the house. He was nearly there when the rain caught him. Eyes narrowed, he made the last few yards at a dead run.

With the sound of the wind and the clashing of the leaves of the oaks in her ears, Sherry had not heard Marie approach. Now the housekeeper moved forward, an anxious tone in her voice as she spoke to her husband. Jules wiped his face on his shirtsleeve before he answered. His tone was grave, his nod back in the direction of the low-hanging clouds over the lake. That their exchange concerned the weather was obvious.

A burst of wind drove rain in upon them in a spattering sheet. Marie gave a small cry and, swinging around, began to slam the wooden storm shutters closed over the long French windows of the house, barring them on the outside. Jules sprang to help her with Sherry close behind. Still, even as she worked, Sherry did not lose sight of the boat near the edge of the lake. Lying there, slowly filling with water, it represented transportation away from Bayou's End — and freedom.

12

Marie was disturbed when Sherry elected to retire to her room instead of staying with her and Jules. The housekeeper seemed to think it was brave but foolhardy of her to prefer the big house to the snug comfort of the small brick kitchen. Sherry finally settled the question by shaking her head with a smile, going into her bedroom, and closing the door behind her. For a few minutes she could hear the sound of Marie and Jules's voices coming from the living room where they had retreated from the fury of the storm, then they faded back toward the rear of the house.

The rain slashed down and the wind rushed at the house in a furious assault. A darkness like night closed down, darkness that, combined with the shutters over the windows, made it impossible to see without turning on the overhead lights, and these flickered and dimmed as if they would go out any moment.

Sherry took out her suitcase and began to pack, carefully searching out everything that she had brought with her. She would not leave so much as a hairpin behind. Though she locked her handbag in one of her suitcases for safekeeping, she left a light all-weather coat and a head-scarf out on the bed. Ready at last, she put on the coat and tied the scarf over her hair, then picked up her two cases and set them out into the living room. She would have to leave by the front door since this was the only one left unshuttered. For a long moment she stood with her hand on the knob, listening.

The sound of the wind seemed to be lessening, the storm dying away. It was now or never.

With a suitcase in each hand she hurried down the steps, taking care not to slip on the wet surface. At the foot she paused for an instant, then made a dash for the boat, her coat flapping and her sandaled feet splashing over the already soaked ground.

With one foot she tilted the light skiff, letting the water slosh out over the side before she flung her bags into it. Wincing at the hollow thud they made against the metal, she pushed the boat out into the water and, just as it cleared the bank, stepped in. She made her way carefully back to the rear seat just in front of the outboard motor. Ducking her head against the rain already plastering her scarf to her head, she caught the rubber handle, staring at the controls. It had been years since she had run one of these, but after her bout with the cruiser the other day she was sure she could do it.

She put the shift lever in neutral, set the control on the handle to start, then she pulled on the rope with all her strength. Nothing happened. A chilling fear that the motor was too wet gripped her. Stilling her nerves, she forced herself to think. The choke, she thought, but before she tried to find it, she gave the rope another pull. Like a loyal friend it burst into life.

The noise racketed around her and she glanced back over her shoulder, expecting to see Jules run from the back of the house. Not that it mattered. With the gap between boat and shore widening by the minute, there was little he could do. Quickly she pushed the lever into reverse, backing out away from the bank far enough for maneuvering room. Then she shifted to forward, turning the throttle for more gas as the motor threatened to stall.

It caught and the boat headed toward the bayou.

She had made it; she had escaped from Bayou's End, and this time there was no possibility of being stopped at the last moment. Exhilaration bubbled in her veins like wine as she bounced over the choppy waves toward the calmer waters of the bayou. Nothing could stop her.

Rain spattered the water around her like a thousand tiny pistol shots and splashed in the bottom of the boat. Her feet were soon covered with water, but she did not care. Ignoring the discomfort, she concentrated on what she had to do. Since she could not see very far ahead, she took it fairly slow until she slid beneath the overhanging trees of the bayou that broke the vicious swipe of the rain. After that she speeded up.

She watched the banks slide past, running with muddy rivulets like thousands of tiny waterfalls. Twigs with green leaves clinging, bits of bark and moss and other fine debris littered the surface of the water. The rain slackened a bit and the trees overhead, their leaves and bark looking fresh washed and new, spattered her with huge drops as she passed beneath them. A windless quiet pressed down, though high overhead the dark clouds still rolled. As Sherry stared about her, an odd shiver ran over her that had nothing to do with the water trickling from her hair.

A low whistling sound made itself heard above the motor's roar. The tops of the trees began to sway. The silt-yellow water rushing past began to be pocked by rain once more. And then in a rush the storm was back. Wind buffeted the boat, making its course erratic as Sherry fought to keep her hold on the control. Tree branches creaked, bowing toward the water.

Through a fog of rain and flying debris, she saw ahead of her a place where the bayou divided. The right leg was wider, more open. She swung that way automatically although she could not remember how Lucien had gone the night before. On their trips they had taken sometimes one fork, sometimes the other.

Her scarf slipped back on her head, and her wet hair was flicked by the wind across her face. She thrust it back, wiping the rain from her eyes. She could feel water creeping down the back of her neck, soaking her dress. Her breathing was deep and labored, as though she had run every step of the way she had come from Bayou's End. Still, despite these things, despite a niggling fear of the wild weather that she could not suppress, she was aware of the primitive attraction of the bayous. The rain streaming from the Spanish moss, the varied colors of green and gray, the hint of hidden danger, the thrashing palmettos, the wild grasses bent and broken by the wind, the swift-moving water, all contributed to the sense of dark, mysterious beauty. In the short time she had been here, it had taken a grip on her imagination from which she was not certain she would ever be free.

After a time Sherry began to peer ahead, thinking that at any moment she should come upon Lottie and Toto's house squatting in the rain with its rickety dock reaching out into the water. There was nothing to see but the twisting rain-drowned banks, nothing to hear but the pelting of the rain. The malignant thought entered her mind that she might not be able to find Lottie's place on this winding bayou with its many branching channels. The few miles' distance between the houses that Lottie had mentioned might have meant anything, straight across country or even the use of some Cajun short cut. There were no highway markers to aid or encourage her. And yet, regardless of whether she found the house where she had attended the *fais-do-do* or not, somewhere along these bayous must live the dozens of other guests who had attended.

There had to be a settlement, houses; it could not all be deserted wetland.

Once again the channel ahead of her diverged and, after a second's hesitation, she swung again to the right. It seemed that New Orleans must lie in that direction somewhere, and she followed that instinct again and yet again as the waterways converged, merged, and divided. She had nothing else to guide her.

At last she allowed herself to think of what she would do if she did not find someone to help her. She was growing chilled and her clothes clung wetly to her. This last waterway seemed narrow, more narrow than any she had traveled so far. Was it possible for her to become so lost back here in this back country that she could not find her way out? Did it matter? She would brave anything, even becoming lost, before she would go back to face Lucien in his sarcastic anger. He would not like it that she had taken Jules' boat, and he would be furious when he discovered she had run away from him.

Or would he? It was all too likely that he would be glad to find her gone. It would save him the trouble of convincing her she had no choice except to return to St. Louis. He would not have to explain the hopelessness of her position to her, or enumerate all the reasons why it would be better if she did not contact Paul. It would, in fact, eliminate a great deal of bother for him. Perhaps the best revenge, if that was what she wanted, would have been to stay at Bayou's End and force him to use all his carefully designed arguments, to let him take her back to New Orleans with every show of meek compliance, and then to turn the tables on him, revealing to Paul and his mother everything that had happened.

It was too late for that. In any case, she did not think she could stand seeing Lucien again, being in his company, having to endure the touch of his mouth on hers. All she wanted was to get as far away from him as she could. The first thing she would do when she reached St. Louis would be to contact a lawyer to have this marriage, if it was one, annulled. Her second act would be to give notice at her job. With those two things behind her, she hoped she would then never hear the name of Villeré for the rest of her life.

There was Paul, of course. She supposed she owed him some sort of explanation. And yet she hated the thought of seeing him. How could he help but remind her of Lucien, of Bayou's End, and of the week she needed desperately to pretend had never happened?

Lightning crackled overhead and thunder shook the sky. The sound jerked Sherry from her absorption. Brushing raindrops curiously warm and salty from her lashes, she gazed skyward. Blue-black clouds hung just overhead. Outlined against them, the tops of the trees leaned away from the gale-force wind that had increased to a banshee wail. A thrill of apprehension swept through her as lightning seemed to split the heavens, followed by the deafening thunder that indicated its nearness.

Sherry flinched, ducking her head in a natural reflex action. Her eyes were closed no more than an instant, and yet when she looked up again, there, dead ahead of the boat, was a sawyer, a half-submerged tree limb. She tried to swerve, but it was too late. The boat plowed into the branches. There was a crackling, rending sound, and then the shaft of the motor struck. The boat swung broadside, was caught by the rain-swollen current and overturned.

It happened so quickly that Sherry had no time to cry out or hold on. The throttle was ripped from her grasp and she was flung from the seat into the cold water, which caught her, pulling her down, washing thick and brown over her head. Her coat dragged at her arms, and her sandals felt like weights on her feet. For endless seconds shock held her in its grip until with a convulsive movement she began to fight her way upward. After an eternity she broke the surface. She coughed, choking as she tried to breathe and tread water at the same time. Clearing her air passages, she opened burning eyes to stare dazedly around her, thrashing about, looking for the bank. Seeing the wash of green through the fogging rain, she began to swim toward it. No matter how hard she tried, however, she seemed unable to gain distance. Her arms were like lead, so heavy she could barely thrust them forward. The coat — she would have to get rid of it.

It was not easy. The material clung with a leechlike hold and once, with the sleeves peeled down over her elbows so she could not move her arms, she thought it was determined to drown her. At last she was free of it. With the last of her strength she swam the few strokes to an exposed tree root dangling in the water. There she clung, her breath rasping hurtfully in her chest. Looking back, she could see the overturned boat half submerged, drifting away from her. The motor was no longer on it, nor was it on the tree limb.

It had sunk without a trace.

There was nothing she could do. She lacked the strength to go after the boat. She watched in numb helplessness as the wind and current sent it against the bank for a moment, then pushed it on out of sight beyond a turn.

Then as lightning flashed again she became aware of the coldness of the water dragging at her sodden skirts, and of the chill of the wind on her wet skin. She must do something, find some kind of shelter.

She kicked out, realizing as she did so that she had lost her sandals. Her effort gained her the trunk of a small sapling and she pulled, dragging herself from the tenacious clutches of the bayou.

Avoid tall trees during lightning. That bit of sage advice passed through her mind and she found herself laughing in grim irony. There were trees all around her. It was impossible to get away from them. Still, she moved as far as possible from the tallest cypresses. Shelter from the wind was her greatest need. Hugging her arms against her chest, she pushed beneath the low-hanging branches of a broadleafed shrub.

She sank down and drew her legs up, huddling into herself, aware even beyond her closed eyelids of the constant flicker of lightning and the continuous thunder like the roaring of jets breaking through the sound barrier. The leaves about her were little protection. The rain spattered through in a fine penetrating mist and the wind found her. She was cold with a deep internal chill, unable to control the convulsive shivers that ran over her.

She could not stay here. It would only be a matter of time before she died from exposure. Perhaps she would be warmer if she moved about. She got clumsily to her feet, her legs stiff. She could move very little however. Undergrowth choked the edges of the bayou, and there was nothing but an impenetrable swamp behind her.

She could not remain still. She slapped her arms, wishing she had on anything other than her thin sundress. She peered through the rain at the windswept bayou. Though it seemed impossible, it appeared that the storm was rising rather than blowing itself out. Could it be a hurricane, one of those devastating gulf storms she had heard so much about? Leaves torn from the trees swirled in the air. Behind her in the woods the branches of the trees creaked and groaned protestingly, while the rushing of the wind flapped her wet dress against her legs and tore at her hair. She tried to pace, but the wind kept throwing her off balance, and finally she leaned against the stout trunk of a tree, sheltering behind its thickness. When she grew too weary to stand any longer she sank to her knees and leaned her throbbing head against its rough bark. She could sense, waiting somewhere at the edge of her mind, a specter of enveloping darkness. It seemed warm, and as it crept closer it was almost welcome. Her body felt heavy, drugged with cold and beaten by the elements. As the moments passed and the shrieking of the gale increased, her mind began to feel light, as though it might be swept away.

And then from out of the drowning rain appeared a white cruiser. It moved silently, a ghost ship easing slowly past, its sound caught up in the storm.

The leap of recognition within her was so powerful that it sent a shock of life speeding through her veins. She opened her mouth to cry out, then the pain and anger she had felt when she had learned that Lucien had made her his wife without her knowledge came rushing back to strike her mute.

She pulled herself to her feet. For a long moment she stood leaning against the tree while the blood tingled in her cramped legs and feet.

Abruptly the boat stopped for a long moment just downstream, then as a light gleamed on the boat, a spotlight that began to sweep the bank, she plunged into the woods. After a few short yards she stopped, her heart pounding in her chest. Perhaps he had not seen her and would pass on by. And yet, what else could have made him stop?

The subdued roar of a motor came to her ears and she caught a flash of white nearing the bank. Faintly against the wind she heard a hail that sounded like her name.

Give up at once or try to run? That was the choice. But where could she run? And so she stood still, outlined against the wet leaves, a wood nymph caught in midflight with rain streaming from her long hair.

When he saw her he stopped. She lifted her chin, an unconscious gesture of defense against the dark fury that drew his brows together. As he moved toward her with a dangerous velvet tread she fought down an absurd desire to placate him with a smile.

His hands closed hard on the chilled flesh of her upper arms. She swayed. Her name on his lips sounded strange, faraway. In a curious, disembodied way she was aware of the raindrops jeweling his thick brows and of his hair plastered in satanic spikes to his forehead.

With a painful intensity she could feel the warmth emanating from his body even through the rain slicker that he wore. Through lips that were stiff and blue-tinged with cold she whispered one word that held both gladness and despair.

"Lucien—"

She floated, her eyes closed, not quite conscious. A rough shake made her open her eyes. She was in the cabin of the boat. Lucien's face was close to her own, his lips near her ear so that she could hear over the drumming of the rain on the deck above them.

"I've got to go back out to tie the boat down better so it can't drift and foul the propellers. Beside you is a blanket. Get out of those wet things and wrap it around you. Now, I'll be back in a minute."

Before she could reply he was gone. With stiff fingers she removed her clothes. They were clammy wet and it was obvious that she would be chilled as long as she was wearing them. She found a small towel near the sink and tried to dry her hair a bit with it before wrapping it turbanlike about her head. She folded the soft warmth of the thermal blanket about her before dropping weakly back onto the bunk and leaning against the wall behind it, drawing her feet up.

She opened her eyes as Lucien entered the cabin once more. He crossed at once to the small galley cabinet and took down a bottle. Pouring a stiff measure of bourbon into each of two glasses, he handed one to her without a word before tossing off his own.

She drank hers, locking her jaws as the heat shuddered over her, watching as he stripped off his slicker and tossed it over a bench.

Balancing himself in the rocking, swaying interior of the cabin, he took her empty glass from her nerveless hand and placed it in the tiny sink. That done, he dropped down beside her.

Again he moved close to be heard. "We won't try to make it home until this" – he waved a hand in a comprehensive gesture – "blows itself out. We can't make any headway against the wind."

She nodded her comprehension, not trusting herself to speak, trying to get a grip on herself, to control the tremors that ran over her in sudden waves. She could feel the warmth of the spirits she had drunk warming her, but it could not touch the ice that lay in her heart.

Suddenly the wind hit the boat with the shuddering force of a solid blow. She lurched forward as the boat swung, unable to save herself with her arms wrapped inside the blanket. Lucien reached to catch her, holding her against his chest as, off balance, they sprawled back into the bunk. He locked his arms around her to protect her as the boat rocked violently. While the storm howled outside she slowly relaxed, and as warmth pervaded her body she ceased to resist the comfort of his embrace.

Beneath her cheek was the firmness of his shoulder and against her forehead the slight roughness of his chin. As if he sensed her submission, Lucien turned to her, his lips finding hers in the dimness. They tasted of the freshness of the rain, the vibrant life of the torrent around them. She closed her eyes, feeling the swirling onrush of a fatalistic content.

As he felt her lips grow softer, her body more pliant, his arms tightened. He brushed a kiss across her silken eyebrows, then with firm and deliberate control he allowed the tension of desire to seep from his clasp. At last he held her with nothing more than the need to protect her against the bruising she would have received as they were thrown from side to side.

Such consideration should have pleased her; it did not. She felt instead the invasion of a feeling like dread. Her punishment when she angered him had so often been a caress that she did not want. What form would it take now that he no longer found her desirable?

Then, as dread turned to desolation, a knowledge that she could not reject however much she tried came to her. It had not been Lucien she had been running from, or even his treatment of her. The thing she had been trying so desperately to outdistance was her love for him.

She lay very still, afraid in those first minutes of realization that she would somehow communicate her newfound understanding to him. She grew uncomfortably aware of his closeness, of his breath fanning her forehead and the steady beat of his heart beneath her hand. Her throat ached with the rise of tears she must not shed, and she took deep, ragged breaths in an effort to hold them at bay.

"Are you all right? Are you hurt?" Lucien murmured.

"No," she managed to answer him. "I'm fine." But it was not so.

13

She was tired, so tired. The emotional strain of the last few days, her exhausting struggle in the water, and the warmth creeping over her combined with the bourbon in her bloodstream to produce a deep languor. The crashing roar of a tree falling somewhere nearby had no power to frighten her. She felt safe, shielded from danger by the dark buccaneer who had come for her out of the storm. A faint giddiness moved over her. She turned her face against Lucien's chest, entwining her fingers in the material of his shirt. Let him think what he pleased, so long as he continued to hold her. If they lived, or if they drowned in the fury of the storm to be swept out to sea and found in each other's arms with seaweed in their hair like mythological lovers, this moment in time would not come again. She did not care if the storm ever ended.

But it did, inevitably. The wind died, the lightning faded to a glimmer on the horizon, the thunder rumbled away and did not return. Though the rain still fell steadily, it had lost its angry lash. Deep in the sleep of utter weariness, Sherry did not know it.

The cabin cruiser rocked gently. From overhead came the patter of gentle rain. Slowly Sherry opened her eyes. Though the light in the cabin was brighter than it had been, it was still tinted with gray. There was one other difference. She was alone in the bunk.

Clutching the blanket about her shoulders, she sat up. By stretching, she could just reach the curtain that covered the porthole at the end of the bunk. She twitched it aside, then drew in her breath, a sharp sound in the quiet cabin.

The cruiser was no longer on the bayou. It was docked at what appeared to be a modern marina. All around her was nothing but boats, cabin cruisers for the most part, sitting in their berths in two long uneven lines connected by a wooden catwalk on pilings. At the far end was a large building like a restaurant or clubhouse. A long hard look convinced Sherry that it was familiar, though the buildinging and marina had been in darkness the last and only time she had ever seen them. This was the place from which she had left New Orleans with Lucien a week before.

Sherry dropped the curtain. That night Lucien had left his car in storage to be used on his return trips. It did not make sense that he would be above decks now in the rain. No doubt he had taken the car and gone, where and why she could not begin to guess. Another, more important question was why he had left her here, alone.

Galvanized by a sudden thought, she swung her legs off the bunk and stood up. The weakness that flooded over her was a surprise, and she caught at the edge of the bunk for support. After a moment it began to pass, allowing her to make her way to the small cabin door. It was locked. She stood with her hand on the knob, turning it back and forth for long seconds before she realized that the locking mechanism was on the inside. Lucien must have snapped it into place on his way out. A simple flick of her thumb and the door came open with ease.

Her relief was great; still it took her no more than an instant to realize that it was premature. Lucien would not expect her to go far wrapped only in a blanket. From all appearances he had taken her clothes, wet and muddy as they were, with him.

Her brows knit in perplexity, Sherry dropped back down on the edge of the bunk. She reached up, running her fingers through her hair. At some time while she was sleeping, she had lost the towel that had been wrapped around it, or else it had been taken away. The long strands were matted together in thick tangles. It was all she could do to force her fingers through them. What she wouldn't give for a deep hot bath and a bottle of shampoo!

The lift of her arm had made her blanket slip. She was no longer as cold as she had been. To secure her covering a little better, she wrapped the soft folds about the upper part of her body just under her arms, tucking the end in place between her breasts to hold it. She could not achieve the proper tension without moving her long chain with the Villeré ring still on it out of the way.

Modesty preserved, she sat turning the ring in her fingers. Soon she would have to part with it. It had never been hers to keep; she had always known that, and yet, she could not help the pain the thought gave her. But then, did it matter? A blue forget-me-not. How could she ever forget?

The sound of approaching footsteps brought her erect. As they thudded on the deck overhead, she dropped the ring and pushed back her hair. By the time the knock came on the cabin door, she was on her feet, ready to spring the lock.

Lucien ducked his head as he came through the doorway. His dark gaze raked over her in a quick examination. "You are looking better," he greeted her.

Her lips curved in a wry smile. "If you mean less like a drowned rat, then I suppose so."

"I brought you something to wear," he said, holding out the package he carried under his arm. As she reached to take it, he turned to close the door behind him. "My mother wasn't home. Aimee ran your things through the washer and dryer for me. I'm afraid she pronounced your dress unfit to be worn, but when I told her you were about her size, she threw in a few things she thought might do."

Sherry stared at the package in her hands. He had not taken her clothes to keep her from leaving; he had gone to have them laundered at his home. He would not have done that unless he intended to reveal her presence and her identity. But why? Why now, after all his efforts to keep them secret?

Lucien swung back. "What are you waiting for? There's a hot bath and a late luncheon on tap for us at home. I don't know about you, but I could use both."

"I—I don't understand you," Sherry said, her turquoise eyes dark in her pale face. "Why did you bring me here?"

"Wasn't it what you wanted? You seemed anxious enough to get here."

"It was what I wanted from the moment I left, but you wouldn't let me go before. Why now?"

He looked away, his sun-bronzed face bleak. "Let's just say it seemed better than letting you kill yourself trying to make it on your own."

"I still don't know how you found me," Sherry said, voicing the words through stiff lips, saying the first thing that came into her mind to relieve the tension that was slowly growing in the small cabin. She was uncomfortably aware of her half-dressed state and of Lucien's careful attempts to avoid noticing.

"Luck," he answered succinctly. "I was half-way to the city when I saw the storm warnings flying. I switched on the radio for the details. It was a tropical storm, something only slightly less than a hurricane, that had veered off its course and was heading for the

Louisiana coastline. I left Paul to go on alone, turned around and went back to warn you at Bayou's End. The first thing I was told when I got there was that you had gone out in Jules' fishing boat. I knew you had not taken the regular route back to New Orleans or I would have met you. I began searching the smaller bayous. I would have passed you by without a sign if I hadn't caught sight of your coat in the water, snagged on a tree root, just downstream from where I found you."

Sherry refused to look at him. "I suppose I should thank you for coming after me. I might have died out there alone."

"And you would almost rather I had let you, wouldn't you?" he asked, a strange timbre in his voice.

He would not understand a denial and she could not explain. She gave a short nod.

"So you could see Paul?"

His harsh tone puzzled her. "Yes, I suppose so. I take it you have no objections now?"

"None whatever."

To Sherry there could be only one explanation of his agreement. "You think you have won then, don't you, with your broom marriage. You think that Paul will never believe I didn't go with you willingly or that I didn't know what I was doing."

267

His eyes narrowed. "So you know about that?"

"Lottie told me this morning," she said with a lift of her chin. Though she wanted to be bold and angry as she threw his deceit in his face, her voice came out flat.

Lucien raised one hand, running his fingers through his hair in a harassed movement. "Lottie."

His grim smile flicked Sherry on the raw. "I'm sure she didn't intend to ruin your plans. She's your friend, not mine."

"I thought so until today," he replied.

"Did you expect to be able to keep it a secret then, this Cajun marriage? Wasn't that too much to expect if you intended to use it to be rid of me?"

Why was she repeating that? Was it in the hope that he would deny it? He obviously had no such intention.

He stared at her a moment longer. "There will be plenty of time to discuss such things later. For now, we are expected at my home. If you will just look in the bag and tell me if you have everything, I will wait for you in the car."

It was all there — her underclothing, a pair of pants and a shirt, shoes, a species of raincoat, even a hairbrush and handful of pins.

When Lucien had gone, Sherry spread them out on the bed. For the first time she felt a stirring of curiosity about Paul's childhood sweetheart, the girl who had chosen the things for her. For a meek, gentle young thing, her choices were strange. The black silk pants matched to a black shirt slashed by a diagonal stripe, the spaghetti-strap sandals, the yellow nylon rain poncho complete with its own jaunty yellow hat hinted at a different personality altogether. Sherry began to look forward to meeting Aimee.

Removing the tangles from her hair, Sherry drew it back in a knot low on the nape of her neck, a style which seemed to suit her borrowed finery. The improvement in her appearance caused a corresponding improvement in her spirits. She did not know precisely what Lucien Villeré had in mind, but she felt more equal to it now than she had an hour ago.

As they left the marina behind them, the only sound was the powerful hum of the car's motor and the slapping of the windshield wipers. The rain had decreased to little more than a drizzle. Though the streets ran with water, there was little sign of wind damage. The tropical storm seemed to have passed by the city.

"Everything fit all right?" Lucien asked finally.

Sherry turned from her contemplation of the passing houses. "Surprisingly well except for the sandals. They are a bit large, but I'm grateful to Aimee for the loan, and to you for bringing them to me."

He glanced at her as if he suspected her of sarcasm, but made no reply. After a moment she went on. "Did you go back by Bayou's End this morning after you found me?"

"No. Why?"

"Marie and Jules will think you are still combing the bayous."

He shook his head. "I contacted them by Citizen's Band Radio. There is a base station installed in the outdoor kitchen. Marie likes to keep up with what's going on."

A base station in the kitchen. There might not have been a telephone, but the means of summoning help had been there. So close. Abruptly something fell into place for her. "Marie knew about the storm. There was no need for you to turn back."

"I knew there was that possibility, but I also knew she could not tell you what was happening. In any case, I never said the storm was the only reason I decided to return."

To question him further would betray her

270

intense interest in the answer. She would not give him that satisfaction. A frown between her brows, she turned back to the window.

The Villeré town house was located near the edge of New Orleans on Lake Pontchartrain, one of a number of great houses set back from a wide, clean street like jewels on the green velvet of their lawns with the open expanse of the lake before them. A classic structure of red brick dating perhaps from the early years of the present century, its size, its columned portico and long, shuttered French windows, were certainly imposing. To Sherry's eyes, however, it seemed to lack the mellow grace and symmetry of Bayou's End.

Inside, the impression was one of quiet elegance. Oystershell-white walls and polished wood floors provided a background for jewel-colored Persian carpets and deep cushioned couches in brilliant colors. The light of sparkling chandeliers fell on highly polished furniture. As she passed the main rooms, Sherry caught the gleam of copper ornaments, the sheen of silver bowls filled with flowers that distilled their scent upon the air, and the glitter of crystal pieces with time-smoothed facets.

Without pausing, Lucien led her to a small breakfast room done in shades of soft lemon and tangerine. With its glass-topped table and fern stands placed on either side of a pair of French doors giving access to the gardens, it reminded Sherry of the house she had left that morning. Stepping inside as Lucien continued to the kitchen to hurry their meal, she felt herself begin to relax in almost imperceptible degrees. The room had one other advantage also. It was unoccupied.

They were given seafood gumbo, crusty French bread, and honeydew melon for lunch. The housekeeper, a woman enough like Marie to be her sister except for a command of English, apologized for the scantiness of the fare. The kitchen was busy with preparations for the party for Mam'zelle Aimee, she said. The cook was having a temper tantrum because of the caterers who kept going in and out, getting in his way. Madame Villeré should be back at any moment. She had said plainly that she meant to rest herself an hour or so before the festivities started.

They had reached the coffee stage when they heard the approach of quick footsteps. A slim woman appeared in the doorway. Her hair was black except for a white streak that began at the widow's peak in the center of her forehead. Her face was slightly tanned and liberally etched with laugh lines about her fine dark eyes. Dressed in cool pink linen, she looked comfortable, casual, and undeniably chic.

"Lucien, my son!" she cried, coming forward with a smile. "What have you been doing? I stopped next door just now and I never heard such a tale!"

Lucien got to his feet. "Mother," he said quietly, "I would like you to meet Sherry Mason."

"My dear," the older woman said as she turned to extend her hand, "I can't tell you how happy I am to meet you. I thought I would never see this day. My elder son, you see, has never had time for women. To him they have a proper but small place in the scheme of his life. They have never been allowed to interrupt more important things, such as his work. To hear of him taking a vacation and returning with a young woman, and then running around with a handful of her wet clothing – all she owns mind you – looking for someone to make them presentable – well, it defeats my imagination."

"Mother—*Maman*—" Lucien said.

Madame Villeré looked at her son, then turned back to Sherry. "Am I embarrassing you, my dear? I hope not, because I meant no harm. It is such an odd thing, having something to tease Lucien about. In any case, I am determined to hear all about it. I've been eaten alive with curiosity since the first of the week when our cousin Estelle dropped by and mentioned seeing the two of you together at Antoine's. She described you as a stunning blonde, Sherry, a girl Lucien was so besotted over that he failed to introduce her properly."

Sherry, about to sip her coffee, nearly choked. She could not resist a glance at the man beside her. To her surprise, a smile that might have been called reminiscent curved his mouth.

"You are not going to give up, are you?" he said to his mother. "If the whole story is what you want, that is what you will get."

For an answer, his mother pulled out a chair at the table and sat down, giving him her complete attention.

When Lucien had finished, she sat staring at him. Her smile had disappeared to be replaced by a troubled frown. She looked at Sherry, then back to her son. "This is more serious than I realized. There are still one or two points I don't understand."

"I am sure there are, *Maman*," Lucien said, "but you need not worry your head over them."

"I wouldn't, except I am not sure you

274

understand yourself," she replied, her tone tentative.

He arched a dark brow. "Are you saying you don't think much of my comprehension? Never mind. I assure you—"

The appearance of the housekeeper in the doorway cut his words short. *"Pardon,* M'sieur Lucien," she said. "You are wanted on the telephone."

A small silence reigned when Lucien had followed the housekeeper from the room. It was his mother who broke it, startling Sherry from a hard study of the door through which he had passed.

"You are very quiet," the older woman said. "Don't you agree with what my son said, or is your version of the story different?"

"He—he left out a few details," Sherry agreed. Such as a mistaken idea of her character and her status with Paul, her initial escape attempt, and the scene their first night together when his ardor had only been deflected by the discovery of the betrothal ring.

"I felt sure of it," Lucien's mother answered. "It must have been a frightening experience for you."

"At first," Sherry admitted.

"Ah, but not later? That is good."

There seemed no reply to that. Sherry kept

her eyelids lowered, tracing the pattern of the china of her coffee cup with one finger. After a moment the other woman went on.

"I feel inclined to apologize for my son. He would hate that, I'm sure, preferring to make his own amends. Let me instead encourage you to listen to what he may have to say. Lucien is – how can I say it? – a man of deep feelings, which he hides beneath a hard surface manner. He takes his responsibilities seriously, hence his protective attitude toward Paul. Because of the differences in their age and temperament, Lucien has stood more as a father than a brother to him. In addition, Lucien is a definite person. If he sees something happening he considers wrong, he takes action to stop it; if he sees something he wants, he goes after it."

Sherry lifted wide turquoise eyes to the other woman's face. "Mrs. – Madame Villeré, there is no need for you to be upset. I don't intend to press charges against your son. At this moment nothing could make me happier than to be able to forget this whole thing ever happened. As soon as I possibly can I will go back to St. Louis. I would leave today, except my handbag with my return ticket, my money, my checkbook, everything, was lost when my boat overturned. But as soon as I can get in touch with my bank and make a few arrangements for clothes and return funds, I will go."

Madame Villeré frowned. "There will be no need for that, I'm sure. I believe the least we can do, under the circumstances, is provide your return flight and replace your wardrobe. You will naturally want to see Paul, also. You must have much to say to each other. He will be here for dinner this evening, and for the party afterward. I don't know if Lucien mentioned it to you, but you will attend of course."

"Oh, I don't think so," Sherry began.

"Nonsense. What would you do otherwise? I doubt you will be able to sleep for the noise, and we would all be uncomfortable knowing you were trying to rest upstairs. There is the problem of what you will wear; I must make a call to attend to that right away. If you will trust me to see to it, I will have a few things sent to the house for your approval. Shoes, underwear, night clothing, makeup, and, I think, an assortment of casual wear? Now, is there anything else I can do for you?"

Sherry would have liked to protest further. It seemed however that Lucien and his mother had much in common; they both were quick to assume responsibility, both used to having their own way. For the moment she had little choice except to let them. "There is one thing," she said, taking a deep breath. "I would love a bath."

14

Sherry soaked in the bathtub for what seemed like hours, enjoying the silken warmth of the water and the bath salts and soap scented with damask roses. In the process she discovered bruises and strained muscles she had not known she possessed. Too indolent and contented to search for her shampoo, she used the same rose soap to lather her hair again and again. When she finally rinsed the last vestiges of the foaming suds from her hair under the shower, she felt clean at last.

The housekeeper, when applied to, produced a hand-held hair dryer. With it and the aid of a brush, Sherry was able to see her hair hanging like a shining curtain about her face once more. This done, there was nothing to occupy her. She could dress in Aimee's clothes and return downstairs, but she was certain her hostess was resting, and she had no wish to see Lucien alone. With a bath sheet wrapped around her, she wandered about the room.

The appointments in this guest room were aqua and white. The carpet was so thick she left her footprints in it like tracks in the snow. The velvet bedspread on the extra-wide bed had such a soft shimmer that she hated to touch it. In one end was a grouping of chairs, table, and bookcases, giving the room the feel of a suite. Even here, however, the antique satin of the upholstery appeared more ornamental than useful.

What was she doing here in this room? It was as alien to her as Lucien Villeré himself. She should never have let herself be talked into staying. How could she know what purpose he had in mind? Something had changed his attitude, had set him off on this odd course. A week before, this was the last thing he had wanted, to see her in his home, to have her meet his friends, his mother, Paul, even Aimee. He had gone to great and improbable lengths to prevent it. What had caused him to reverse himself?

Could it be the peculiar marriage ceremony they had gone through together? Was there some significance to it she did not see, or that

Lottie had failed to mention? Could it, in fact, be completely binding, to the point that Lucien was certain she was no longer a threat to Paul's happiness? Still, how could that be the case? If Lucien intended to introduce her into the family as his wife in some sense, and therefore out of Paul's reach, he could not have taken into account the feelings that Paul might well be expected to have at learning his fiancée had been stolen out from under his nose. If Lucien thought Paul would be disillusioned by her fickle and mercenary conduct, there was one thing he had left out of his calculations. He had left it out because it was something he did not know, the essential fact that there had never been an engagement at all between Paul and herself.

Sherry moved to the window, staring down into the garden where Chinese lanterns had been turned on in the gathering gloom. Though the rain had stopped, the light glistened on the wet surface of the brick-paved terrace that led from the rooms on the ground floor at the rear of the house. She drew a sharp breath, holding it against a feeling inside like pain. With sudden passion she wished that, false or not, the arrangement with Paul had never taken place, that she had never seen Lucien, never heard of the jumping of the broom, and never, no never, fallen in love with a pirate.

This somber train of thought was interrupted by a tap on the bedroom door. Drawing her towel closer around her, Sherry moved to answer it. The housekeeper stood outside, her arms piled high with dress boxes and plastic bags emblazoned with the name of one of New Orleans's oldest and most famous department stores. At Sherry's bidding the woman entered and, with a flourish, placed her load on the foot of the bed.

"Here you are, Mam'zelle. Madame Villeré told me of the loss of your wardrobe. Such a terrible thing — except that it calls for a new one, eh? Will you be needing any help with zippers and hooks?"

"No, thank you, I don't think so," Sherry answered, her lips curving in response to the woman's droll friendliness. When the housekeeper had gone, she stood staring at the boxes and bags. It appeared Lucien's mother had ordered an entire store for her approval. At least in that array there should be something she could wear.

The only trouble was, there was too much. Nearly every garment she tried, from long evening dresses to a pair of jogging shorts, fit perfectly. There were three long dresses she could choose from to wear for the party. Sternly putting everything else to one side, she considered them. There was a cherry-red knit, a soft brown voile, and a pale-gray crepe with turquoise shadings. Red had never been her color; it was too vivid, too overpowering. The voile was attractive, but too similar, with its off-shoulder ruffle, to the dress she had worn on the night she and Lucien had met. Gray might not be a festive color, but the hint of turquoise in the folds brought out the color of her eyes, and it seemed, all in all, the closest match to her disposition.

She was buckling the straps of a pair of silver evening sandals when she thought she heard the sound of a sports car on the drive below. It was early yet for guests to be arriving. Paul, however, could not be considered a guest. The thought was not an agreeable one. It was not long afterward that a knock came again on the door. It was Lucien who stood in the opening. In correctly formal evening wear, he seemed cold and withdrawn, a stranger once more. His dark eyes met hers for a tense moment. It might have been a trick of the light, but she thought there was a look of torment in their depths before he glanced away.

"We have time for a drink before dinner, if you are ready," he said.

Nodding, she stepped from the room, closing the door behind her. Together they moved down the hall, their backs straight, their steps in perfect unison. It was almost as if they moved reluctantly toward some dreaded goal, Sherry thought. She was painfully aware of the man beside her, of the tight impassivity of his features, his air of controlled strength and purpose. She felt an odd need to put out her hand to stop him, to call a halt to their grim advance. She did no such thing, but walked on, her chin high and her eyes fixed straight ahead.

With his hand beneath her elbow, they descended the stairs. They crossed a wide, open foyer, passing beneath an enormous brass chandelier which hung from the height of the second story above them, and entered the living room, whose double doors stood open in welcome. Only a series of table lamps lighted the dimness of the long room. They were enough to reveal the look of a reception area left ready for guests with every cushion in its proper place, a supply of ashtrays and coasters ready to hand, and a tray of drinks sitting on a small antique sideboard.

The room was not empty. At their entrance a man turned from the sideboard with a drink in his hand and a welcoming smile on his face.

"Lucien!" he called. "So you did make it back. I was beginning to wonder —" He trailed off as his gaze moved to his brother's companion, then he exclaimed, "Sherry!"

"Hello, Paul," Sherry said. Her lips moved in some semblance of a smile, though her eyes remained bleak.

Paul flicked a glance at his brother before he went on. "I thought you weren't coming."

In some distant corner of her mind, Sherry realized there was scant welcome in Paul's manner. He seemed more than anything else to be disconcerted. It did not matter, of course, but it was peculiar after the way he had pleaded with her only two weeks ago. Even more peculiar was her reluctance to tell him what had happened and his elder brother's part in it. It could not be helped. Her presence had to be accounted for, and that could be done in only one way.

"It seems," she began carefully, "that there was a small change in plans."

"What Sherry is trying to say," Lucien interrupted, his voice harsh, "is that she left St. Louis and arrived in New Orleans a week ago today. She has spent the time since then with me, at Bayou's End."

Paul looked from one to the other. "I don't think I understand."

"I was curious to see this fiancée you had produced so conveniently at such short notice, curious too, to hear her version of the tale without your being present. In the beginning, I meant no more than that, to take her to dinner and to talk. We spent an evening together, and before it was over I could see that you were totally wrong for each other. I made one other discovery also; that she was the kind of woman I might, given time, come to love."

Paul looked at his brother through narrowed eyes. "And so, in your usual high-handed fashion, you talked her into forgetting her agreement with me and going with you to Bayou's End?"

"Agreement? That's an odd term. But no, you have it wrong. I kidnapped her."

"You what?"

"I persuaded her to go with me to Bayou's End, where she thought she would see you, and then I kept her there. Last night we jumped the broom together with half the people of the bayou as witnesses. When the marriage is duly recorded with the clerk of court, she will be my legal wife, though I consider her in that light now."

"I can't believe it," Paul said, his voice low. "You, Lucien, of all people."

Nor could Sherry believe it. There was no

triumph in Lucien's voice, no self-righteous hints of the fate from which he had saved his brother by preventing him from marrying her. Though he had said that she and Paul were unsuited, he had not suggested she was not good enough for him. Quite the opposite, in fact. By allowing it to appear that it was the strength of his desire, rather than of his disapproval, that had caused him to intervene in his brother's engagement, he had made her appear something special. Despite these things, however, Sherry felt a coldness settled around her heart. There had been no need for him to pretend to love her.

"You can believe it or not," Lucien was saying. "That is what happened."

"The telegram I received from Sherry?"

"Arranged by me to be sent from the St. Louis office. Sherry did not want you to worry, and I had no wish for you to come tracking her down like the outraged lover."

Paul turned to set down his glass, then swung back. There was a belligerent look in his dark eyes as he faced his brother. "What in the name of all the saints gave you the idea that you could do a thing like that, and to a girl like Sherry?"

"It was necessary to keep you from announcing your engagement and ruining both your lives."

"Was it? Let me tell you something, my dear brother, since Sherry obviously has not. There would have been no ruined lives because there would have been no marriage. I asked Sherry to be my wife and she refused. I begged her to at least pretend to be my fiancée, and she would not even consider it until your suspicions and high-handed tactics goaded her into it. So you see, Lucien, you did it all for nothing!"

Lucien's head came up, his brows drawn together in a frown. "There was no engagement?"

"Nothing more than an arrangement between friends."

"But she had − has the family ring."

"Only under protest, to appease the evil-minded," Paul said, his voice carrying the lash of sarcasm.

The sudden quiet was broken by a lively hail from the open doorway. "So here is where everyone is? I was beginning to think the house was deserted!"

Consternation flitted across Paul's features and then was gone. With a warning glance at his brother, he turned toward the girl in the doorway. "The guest of honor," he called, "and no one to greet you! That's what you get for slipping in the back way. Come on in, there's someone here I want you to meet."

The dark-haired girl who came down the room toward them was not beautiful in the classical sense, but she had that elusive quality called style. She moved with confidence and an utter disregard for the way she looked to those watching. And yet, the simple, figure-skimming black gown she wore, and the madonnalike severity of her hair drawn back from a center parting, were perfect. Closer inspection revealed no faults. Her manner, though polished, was unaffected, and her smile charm itself. It was easy to see why there was a special light in Paul's eyes as they rested upon Aimee Dubois.

As the introductions were made, Sherry tried to thank the other girl for the loan of her clothing.

"Please think nothing of it," Aimee said. "Since I've been in similar situations once or twice, I was glad to be of help."

"Oh you have, have you?" Paul asked. "I'd like to hear more about this!"

"Would you?" Aimee replied. "I might consider it if you have some amusing story to tell in return."

Paul pretended to search his memory. "I'll

289

make something up," he offered in mock innocence.

"Not good enough," Aimee jibed. "Please don't let me interrupt your conversation, however. I had the distinct impression that my arrival called a halt to something interesting."

Paul glanced from Sherry to his brother. "We wouldn't dream of boring you with it," he answered, a shade too quickly.

Aimee's sprightliness left her to be replaced by genuine contrition. "I'm sorry. Shall I go away again?"

It was Lucien who answered. "Not," he said deliberately, "unless you take Paul with you."

Stepping to Paul's side, Aimee tucked her hand into the crook of his arm. "You heard the man," she said. "Come along and I will show you the gardens by lantern light. Whatever the problem is, you will find me a sympathetic listener."

Paul hesitated, his gaze going to his brother's forbidding face. "Why is it," he complained, "that I have the feeling I am being thrown to the wolves?"

"Wolf," Aimee corrected with a demure smile.

Paul's dilemma was plain. He wanted very much to remove Aimee from this room where she might inadvertently learn that he had tried to hide from their past attachment behind a false engagement to another woman. At the same time he did not like leaving Sherry to face his brother's wrath over his revelation alone. The only one who could release him was Sherry herself. She did so with a strained smile and a shake of her head. An apology in his eyes, Paul let himself be led away.

Lucien, his expression shuttered, watched this byplay. When the couple had passed out of sight, he spoke, his voice quiet, almost reflective. "So there was no engagement?"

"No."

"I should have known – I did know – but you confused me; you still do. Why? I don't understand why."

"Paul told you," she said, her words clipped as he moved closer.

"He told me why you agreed in the first place, not why you went through with it."

"I had given my word."

"Yes, you had given your word to Paul. But didn't you realize the way it made you appear – a gold-digger, and worse?"

"I was not responsible for the false impression you had of my character and morals."

"But admit you did nothing to correct it. You even, unless I miss my guess, set out at our first meeting to prove me right!"

She looked away, a flush tinting her cheekbones. "You were certain you knew precisely what I was and what I was after. You had set yourself up not only as my judge, but as the final word on what was best for me and for Paul."

"And for the sake of your pride and the pleasure of thumbing your beautiful nose at me, you came extremely close to paying the full price. Do you realize," he demanded, his voice vibrant with anger, "how much I wanted you, and how near I came to taking what I wanted?"

As she turned away from him, away from the suppressed passion burning in his eyes, he reached out and caught her arm. His fingers seemed to scorch the flesh beneath the crepe sleeve of her dress. "You could have stopped me with a word," he went on, "but you wouldn't open your mouth. Why? Were you still trying to protect Paul from his own stupidity?"

Stung, Sherry swung on him, her blue eyes clashing with his darker gaze. "I could have stopped you with a word? How was I to know that, when it seemed the fact that I was promised to your brother held no meaning for you? You had already shown how cheap you held me; how was branding myself an imposter supposed to help?"

"You could have worn the Villeré ring instead of hiding it like something you were ashamed of. Deny, if you can, that it had no effect."

Sherry dropped her gaze to the pulse that throbbed in his throat. It had been the ring and its apparent proof of her relationship with his brother that had caused Lucien to draw back when he might have possessed her. "It was not mine, I – I had no right to wear it."

"No," he agreed. "Nor do I think you will ever have that right for my brother's sake. In that much, at least, I was correct. Paul and Aimee belong together."

"Yes, I'm sure you are right," she said, her voice low. With trembling fingers she drew the long chain holding the betrothal ring from her bodice and pulled it off over her head. "Here, he will need this, and I would rather not have the responsibility for it any longer."

Lucien made no offer to take it. "Such self-sacrifice in the name of love. I must remind you, however, that you are still my promised wife, if not something more. That being the case, I think it is time we dispensed with this."

Taking the fine gold necklace in his hand, he stripped the ring from it, then dropped the chain into his pocket. Reaching for her left hand, he slid the ring onto her finger. She tried to draw her hand away, but he held it tightly clasped in his.

Reluctantly she raised her eyes to his. "Why are you doing this? Why have you brought me here, and why do you insist on making what happened between us public?"

"Call it a gamble," he answered, his face set in tight lines.

"But why go on with it?" she insisted, a trace of desperation in her tone. "So far only your mother knows, and Paul. Don't you realize it may be over between Paul and Aimee if she discovers why I came, why you took me to Bayou's End? The longer I stay, the more likely it is everything will come out."

"What does it matter to you?" he asked.

If she told him, he would not believe her. She pressed her lips firmly together before she answered. "Nothing. Nothing at all."

"Then you may as well see the final outcome. After the part you have played, it would be a shame if you missed it."

Dinner was a trying meal, an hour dedicated to platitudes, meaningless smiles, and endless small talk. It was not a large gathering. Other than Madame Villeré, Sherry and Lucien, and Paul and Aimee, there was Madame Dubois,

Aimee's grandmother, and Étienne and Estelle Villeré. On closer acquaintance, they seemed an amiable pair. Their air of congeniality was so pervasive, however, that she could not decide whether they had in truth mistaken Lucien's motives for failing to introduce her at their first meeting or whether they had simply put the best possible face on the encounter when speaking of it to his mother. Whichever version represented the truth of the matter, social blindness or a kind heart, Sherry was inclined to like them for it.

Paul, she thought, had a subdued look about him. Though she had not known Aimee long enough to recognize her moods, Sherry did not think the girl was any different from when she had first met her earlier in the evening. With a fund of small talk which did not depend too conspicuously on the tropical storm that had passed over during the morning, she did her part to assist her hostess in keeping the conversation moving.

Nor did the Creole girl flag as the evening progressed. As the house filled with people and the crowd overflowed out into the garden, she was everywhere. Laughing, scintillating groups of people crowded around her. She would stay for a time talking in vivacious animation, and then with a quip she would be gone to repeat the same scene in another section of the house or gardens. She danced, she ate and drank, but as the evening advanced, Sherry began to notice that Paul was seldom at her side. For some reason the couple was avoiding each other. It did not take a genius to decide what that reason must be.

"Paul?"

Sherry ran him to earth in a dim corner of the garden. The only illumination was the red Chinese lantern that cast an odd pink glow over the white cast-iron garden seat where he was sprawled.

"Hello, Sherry," he answered, his voice tired but still deeper, more mature than she remembered. He sat up straighter, making room for her beside him.

"What are you doing out here?" she asked bluntly. "Why aren't you with Aimee?"

"Why should I be with Aimee?" he countered.

"For the simple reason that it's where you'd rather be."

The pink light slid across his face as he turned to look at her. After a moment he gave a nod. "So I would. You always were a smart girl."

"I take that as a compliment," Sherry said,

then went on. "I suppose you told her about our so-called engagement."

He gave a slow nod. "There wasn't much else to do under the circumstances. She would have heard about it from someone sometime."

"I'm afraid so. I'm sorry for my part in it."

"Don't worry about it," Paul said with a sigh. "I know only too well who is to blame. It isn't you and it certainly isn't Lucien. I brought it on myself, so I guess you could say I deserve it. I just wish Aimee wouldn't take it so hard. I can't take knowing I've hurt her."

Sherry's gaze went to where the Creole girl was dancing on the terrace. She was laughing up at the man who held her in his arms, a man who happened to be Lucien.

"Oh, I know what you're thinking," Paul said. "But Aimee is not the kind of person who parades her feelings, making a lot of noise for the sake of sympathy. In that, she reminds me of you, Sherry."

"It's kind of you to say so," Sherry said, swallowing over a sudden fullness in her throat.

"I didn't say it to be kind," Paul replied. "I said it because I saw the way you looked at my precious older brother this evening."

She glanced at him, then looked quickly away again. "I don't know what you mean."

"Don't you? I warn you. I'm more than ordinarily sensitive to that sort of thing these days."

Sherry tried for a light laugh that did not quite come off. "It's so stupid, falling in love with a man like that. The sooner I get away from here the better it will be."

"Are you afraid of him?"

"No, nothing like that," she answered, so much surprise in her tone that he had no choice but to accept it.

"Women are forgiving," he commented.

"Are we?" she queried, then added with a significant nod at the girl on the terrace. "Possibly, if we have reason to be."

"Reason being love?" Paul said. Without waiting for an answer, he went on. "Feeling that way about Lucien, are you certain it's wise to leave just now?"

"I have to," she said with a short nod. "The only trouble is, I can't."

"Because of the loss of your belongings?"

"I'm afraid so. No money — no ticket."

"If that's all it is, I may be able to help."

She swung toward him, a look of strain in her sea-blue eyes. "Could you, Paul, without going through Lucien's office or the shipping line?"

"The offices are closed for the weekend," he

answered, his tone vague, as though his mind were busy with other things. After a moment he gave an abrupt nod. "Tomorrow is Sunday, but if I came and picked you up early in the morning, you should be able to make connections for St. Louis."

"Oh, Paul," Sherry said, reaching out to clasp his arm. "I can't tell you how much it would mean to me. I'll pay you back, every penny."

"No, forget it," he answered, a sudden sharp note in his voice. "It's the least I can do after the problems I caused you."

The remainder of the evening passed quickly. Secure in the plan she and Paul had worked out together, assured that she was at last going to gain control of her life, Sherry was able to relax. She even managed to enjoy herself in a quiet way. She danced with Paul, with Étienne Villeré and finally with Lucien. The last was a bittersweet thing that stirred memories of the only other time they had moved together in time to music, at the *fais-do-do*. It was also a silent farewell. With the same motive she sought out Madame Villeré. She sat for a time chatting with her, then went to look for Aimee, intending to make her apologies once and for all for her part in the deception. There was also in the back of her mind an idea that if the opportunity arose, she might smooth Paul's way.

There was no need. Sherry found the girl in the garden. She was clasped tightly in Paul's arms beneath the pink light of a red Chinese lantern. Turning, Sherry left them alone in the night.

Sherry did not sleep well. Between shortly after one o'clock when the party finally ended, and dawn, she jerked into wakefulness a half dozen times. The clock on the bedside table read only a little after five when she finally gave up the effort and climbed out of bed. Selecting the simplest and least expensive-looking of the casual dresses Madame Villeré had ordered, Sherry put it on. A pair of medium-heeled sandals, a quick bit of attention to her makeup and hair, and she was ready.

Sternly she resisted the temptation to tiptoe out of the house. She was not a prisoner, nor was she, strictly speaking, an invited guest who must take leave of her host. She would have liked to have said good-bye in the normal way to Madame Villeré, but it could not be helped. She would send a short note— No, better to let it seem she was without manners than to have it look as though she were calling attention to her stay.

It was quiet in the house, even in the back areas where the kitchen staff would soon be stirring to clear away the debris left by the party. Unwilling to chance meeting an early riser, Sherry turned in the opposite direction, letting herself out the front door.

The sky was growing lighter in the east. In a short time the sun would begin to creep over the horizon, inundating the land with its warm golden light. As she passed beneath a palm tree that leaned over the driveway, she could hear a pair of mockingbirds chattering in its topmost fronds. Nesting, she thought, and her lips moved in a brief smile. Before the house, Lake Pontchartrain stretched blue-brown and placid with a tugboat pushing a barge just visible on its surface in the uncertain light. Small with distance, they had the look of children's toys too impossibly tiny to be of use.

Halfway down the drive, Sherry realized that she still wore the Villeré betrothal ring. She had meant to leave it behind in her room. Even if she could bear the suspense of returning to the house to leave it, there was no time. Paul had arranged to meet her at the end of the drive in order to keep from rousing the house. Even now she could see his low-slung sports car approaching, gliding toward her. He would be livid if she kept him waiting. Of course. She would give it to Paul for safekeeping. That would be returning it full circle. She quickened her footsteps, a smile of anticipation beginning to form on her mouth.

The car slid to a halt just as she reached the edge of the pavement. The driver leaned across to open the door for her, then drew back. She stepped in and slammed the door. The instant the latch snapped, the car began to move once more in an operation as swift and smooth as if it had been practiced a hundred times.

With a grin of satisfaction and triumph, Sherry turned to the man beside her. Abruptly her elation disappeared, banished by cold disbelief. The man at the wheel was Lucien. As she watched him, he touched the door panel at his left side. With a metallic click, the right car door beside her was electronically locked. Only when that was done did he turn to look at her.

Under the sunburned darkness of his skin, his face was pale and his mouth was set in a straight line. "Good morning, *Chérie*," he said.

"Where are you taking me this time?" she inquired, unable to keep the bitterness she felt from seeping into her tone. "Or am I allowed to ask?"

"First I am taking you to a place where we can talk, and then, if you still want to go, to the airport."

What answer she had expected she could not have said. Still, the one she had been given was not satisfactory. It was a moment before she could recognize the emotion that crept over her. It was disappointment.

"How did you—I suppose Paul told you what I was going to do?"

"I'm afraid so. He had this idea, you see, that you were making a mistake. Correcting mistakes, one way and another, seems to run in the family."

Sherry could not believe it. It made no sense that Paul had given her away. He had only caused her more distress for nothing. Conserving her strength, she did not speak again until the car came to a stop.

They were in the French Quarter. Though they had come by a different route than before, Sherry had recognized its narrow streets and distinctive architecture the instant the car entered the old section. She could see the tall spire of the St. Louis Cathedral and, closer at hand, the long, graceful colonnade of the French market. With a sense of discovery she realized they were only a short walk from the Café du Monde and the scenic walkway over the Mississippi.

Lucien pressed the button which unlocked her door. Sliding out, he came around to open it for her, then slammed it shut behind her. He took her arm, turning in the direction of the river.

A Sunday-morning quiet filled the streets. A truck rumbled past, followed by one or two cars. There were a few customers at the coffee shop, but the river walkway they had to themselves. Lucien strolled a short distance, then stopped, turning to lean on the railing. Sherry moved on another step before she came to a halt also.

It had been dark with the blackness of midnight when she had stood here last. Then she had not been able to see the full majesty of the river. Now she watched the wide, enormous rush of silt-laden water surging past on its way to the gulf. There was something strong, remorseless, and yet benign.

"Why were you running away?" Lucien asked abruptly.

Sherry controlled a start. She had not forgotten Lucien's presence, only his anger. "I asked you to let me go," she answered, "and you refused."

"Had it occurred to you I might have had a reason?"

"Oh, I don't doubt it," she said with a wan smile. "You were sorry you had misjudged me, sorry that you had driven me to half kill myself in order to escape you. You felt there was some reparation due for the way in which Paul had attempted to use me, and you found me — not unattractive."

"That may all be true as far as it goes."

"Don't tell me it doesn't go far enough? Oh, yes, I had forgotten. Given your heritage, I suppose it is entirely possible that you might have felt some impulse of honor, the need to restore my good name by replacing it with yours."

For the first time, a smile curved Lucien's mouth. "A romantic notion, but I am not quite that steeped in tradition. Will you listen to me now?" At her reluctant nod, he went on. "I think you know what I thought of you when we left from this spot a week ago. I had a preconceived idea of you as a goodtime girl, out for the fun, ready for the sake of an airline ticket and a week's holiday in New Orleans to pretend to be Paul's fiancée. To be sure, you were more intelligent, more sensitive than most, but it was still the only explanation that fit the facts as I knew them.

What's more, I was attracted to you, more entranced than I could ever remember with a woman at a first meeting. It was that last discovery, as much or maybe more than a need to separate you from Paul, that tipped the scales in favor of Bayou's End. I thought a few hours, a few days, would be enough to give me a surfeit of your charms."

The harsh ring of truth was in his voice. Sherry stood still, hardly daring to breathe as he went on.

"I was wrong. I found myself watching you in fascination, enjoying raising your temper, waiting for your smile. I wanted you as I have never wanted another woman. And then I discovered what I took to be proof that you belonged to my brother. I came back to New Orleans. I questioned Paul about you without letting him know that I had seen you. He was cagey. Even then, when he had your telegram and knew you weren't coming, he still pretended the engagement was real. I suppose he didn't want to admit to me that he had lied. I knew him well enough to be certain his feelings were not too much involved, but I could not trust him to stay uninvolved if you were put in his way again. If he saw you and decided to make your engagement public I would have been honor bound not to interfere.

There was no other way; you had to stay with me. I went back to Bayou's End with a little more insight into your character, but also with the knowledge that I had given you reason to hate me. Looking at you, so soon after coming from Paul, I knew you were not right for him, nor was he right for you. I could not help but realize, however, that by my actions I had destroyed my own chances. Given time, the damage might have been mended, but time was limited. I knew our idyll on the bayou could not last, knew we would not be left long in peace. I knew also that at the first chance you would go as far away from me as you could. If I ever wanted to claim you as mine, then I had to bind you to me in some way."

"And so the *fais-do-do*," Sherry said, her voice low.

"To me, the commitment I made that night was as sacred as though it had been spoken in the cathedral yonder, before a priest, and just as valid a symbol of the love and honor I felt for you."

Lost in contemplation of the memory of that bayou ceremony, and afterward, of the way he had made love to her and his restraint, it was a moment before what he had said made an impression. "Love?" she asked,

307

swinging to face him. "How can you speak of love when the next morning you left me to come back to New Orleans, to Aimee's party, as though I didn't exist?"

A black scowl drew his brows together. "What makes you think I came back for the party? If it had been only that I would never have left Bayou's End. No, Paul came for me because of a business emergency, the same matter that kept me occupied yesterday afternoon. Even so, if you will remember, I turned back, and not only for the storm. I turned back because I had gathered from what Paul had said of Aimee that they were beginning to recapture what had been between them so many years ago. That being so, I could not bear to leave you behind. I wanted everything open and above board, with it fully understood that you belonged to me."

"Oh, Lucien," she said, pain threading her soft tone.

"You should pity me," he said, "for you will never know what I endured searching for you in the storm, knowing that if you died I was to blame, that my arrogant rearranging of your life was the cause of it."

"Don't, please don't," she said, drawing nearer to touch his hands, clenched so tightly on the railing that his fingertips were white.

"It would not have been true. It wasn't what you had done or even the way you had treated me that made me run away. I was running from myself, from the love I felt for you, and from the pain of thinking that you had been playing with me, that to you it had all been a game."

As if released by her touch from his rigid self-control, he turned and swept her into his arms. His mouth found hers and clung in a kiss that was tender in its possessiveness. She molded her body to his, offering wordlessly the most effective solace for pain – love.

With an unsteady laugh Lucien loosened his hold. "Sherry – *Chérie,*" he breathed, brushing his lips against the soft hair at her temple. "So you do love me?"

"More than I can say. I have been so unhappy, lying to you, deceiving you."

Lucien gave an unsteady laugh, his breath warm against her temple. "When Paul told me last night there had never been an engagement, I didn't know whether to half kill him for it or shake his hand for relieving me of the guilt of taking the woman he loved. And then, just as I was beginning to realize my luck, I saw the way you looked at him and it occurred to me you might be in love with Paul. As a final insult you tried to give me back the ring. The only thing that kept me from losing my mind was the feeling I had deep inside that you belonged to me. And then last night, or early this morning, Paul redeemed himself by giving me a strong hint of how you felt and offering me his place as your taxi to the airport."

"The traitor," Sherry murmured. "He just wanted to make certain I wasn't around to plague him."

"So do I," Lucien said, his hands gentle as they smoothed over her back. "I know a doctor who would open his office to give us a blood test this morning as a special favor. We could be married in seventy-two hours."

"We could?"

"After that we could go anywhere you wanted, anywhere in the world."

"Could we?"

He drew back, staring down at her bemused face and the radiance in her turquoise eyes. The grip of his fingers on her arms tightened a fraction. "I have not, I know, made my proposal in the most romantic fashion, but if I followed the inclination of my blood and the example of at least one of my ancestors, I would tell you flatly that I am going to have you regardless of what you want. The instant you were legally mine, I would take you to

Bayou's End and keep you there for as long as I could hold the world at bay. And yet, I would prefer a willing bride."

"If it is to be Bayou's End, then you have one," she answered, her eyes dancing with sweet mischief before she closed them and lifted her face for the warm and gentle passion of his kiss.